SILENTLY
INTO
THE
NIGHT

By
Candace Osmond

Candace Osmond

Cover Work by Majeau Designs
Facebook.com/MajeauDesigns

DEDICATION

To my mother.

CHAPTER ONE

"Life asked Death, *why do people love me but hate you?* Death responded, *because you are a beautiful lie, and I'm the painful truth.*" – **Unknown**

The clocks did not stop. No guardian angel took her by the hand. Nor did her life flash before her eyes. The only light in the living room was dappled, orange-red and gloomy; the last slivers of sunset peeking in through her old, nicotine-yellowed window blinds.

Blythe Foley knew death was near, she knew it like she knew the scents that augured in each and every change of the seasons. This smell, in particular, was so specific, so unmistakable, she shuddered at the memory it evoked. She craned her neck to make sure the windows were closed. They were. No way was this an actual smell in the room, then. It was her brain playing tricks on her, prepping her for the end. The book she'd been reading, *The Girl on the Train*, slid off her lap and tumbled onto the carpet.

As she bent to pick it up, a twinge in her left arm drew an old but familiar pain. It tightened like a red-hot piano wire up her arm to her shoulder, where the pain creased and threatened to snap into her chest.

But it didn't. It dissipated.

As Blythe sank back in her favorite armchair, shivering in a cold sweat, gasping for breath, the relief was so strong she started to cry. Yes, she *would* get to say goodbye to Rose and Andy. All she needed was a few more days. So close to the end, the only thing she wanted from life now was to spend a bit more time with her children, no matter how distant they'd been lately. Blythe scooped up her framed photo of the three of them, taken on the last vacation they'd spent together—Palm Springs, summer 2008—and clutched it to her chest. For Pete's sake, *that* was the memory she wanted to take with her, not the one death was insisting she…

"Since when did I insist on anything?"

Blythe sat up, frantically scanning the room. Half of it was wreathed in shadow, the other half held loosely by fingers of cooling light. Outside, the sunset's glare reflected off the windows of neighboring apartments, needling the corner of her eye as she focused on the darkness in front of her.

"Who said that? Who's there?" She motioned toward the phone on her medication table, but a strong knowing feeling deep inside told her it would be dumb to dial for help.

"Don't you know? Have you not been expecting me?"

Again, the pungent, perfumed scent of wet hay mixed with burning motor oil—so specific to that tragic day from her past it took her breath away. That smell and that memory linked inextricably by death.

"Where are you?" she asked.

"Here in your living room."

"Why don't you show yourself?"

There was no reply.

"You should know I don't receive uninvited guests," Blythe said. "Why don't you come back another time, when I'm better prepared?"

"Let me guess. Fifteen years from now? You'll send a postcard when you're ready?"

"Well, I wouldn't know where to mail it, but sure, that sounds like a plan." She swallowed. Cracking wise with death in the room probably wasn't the smartest route to long life, but it was either that or slip away quietly. Blythe had never gone quietly in her life; she had no intention of starting now.

"That accent, that diction; they don't go together," she pointed out. "Texas, but your delivery is stiff and proper. Who are you supposed to be?"

"I never choose the form I take."

"Form?"

He didn't respond. The silence thickened, seemed to charge the air in the room. Together with the pungent scent, it excited the memory of that fateful day at the fair: no longer just the tragic outcome, now she recalled the happiness before it, the love she'd felt, the natural high of just being with all the people she cared about most in this world, all on the same outing, on the same damp, sunny day. Yes, there was love in the room with her, not just death. The scent was a bittersweet one, she realized.

He stepped half out of the shadows, into the cool dusk light that didn't seem to fade.

Blythe squinted to see his face, but her eyesight wasn't what it used to be. She put her glasses on. "You!"

But her reaction was knee-jerk, not backed by any sort of understanding. It was a familiar face she was seeing, but it took her several searching moments to place it, to give a name to the face and a memory to both.

"What are *you* doing here?"

He didn't respond. The minute turn of his head toward the photos on the mantel revealed more of his young features. He was in his mid-twenties, handsome, clean-shaven, with dark brown, almost obsidian eyes that caught the embers of twilight and didn't blink. His long, shoulder-length blond hair, a fashion she'd never really liked on men, despite being a teenager in the 60s, suited him. Less so his cotton shirt, black jacket, and pants, which came off as an ironic ensemble a rebel might wear for his grandma's sake, to hide the fact that his usual wardrobe consisted of biker denim and an MC cut.

Of course, Blythe knew all this to be true because she knew *him*, the boy who'd come to fetch her, the boy whose face *was* death: His. Soon to be hers. It all made perfect sense, and yet she couldn't quite swallow what was happening.

"Thomas Bonden, am I dreaming?"

"You tell me."

"I-I think I must be. This is way too *eerie*."

"And most reality isn't?"

Her hands began to shake. The photo frame slid from her weak grip. Luckily, her tennis days hadn't completely deserted her, those lightning reactions came to the rescue as she caught the picture and stood it on the medication table in one fluid heart-in-mouth motion. The ragged pulse returned to her chest, threatened to spread its tightness. But, several deep measured breaths managed to still it, at least momentarily.

"This is the end, isn't it? I'm out of time."

"Yes."

She dare not look him the eye. Instead, her gaze fixed on his shoes. Cheap but clean brown loafers, exactly what she'd expect Hank Bonden's son to wear on a Sunday outing.

"So, this isn't a dream?" she asked.

"Does it matter?"

"I…I don't know. It seems like one, but it doesn't feel like one."

"People die in their sleep all the time, Blythe. When it arrives, what's the difference?"

"When it arrives? You mean when *you* arrive?"

Again, he didn't respond. Each silence flooded the room with heavy air, the kind that taxed her lungs. She knew she would have to fight if she wanted more time, but perhaps that, too, was futile. Unlike Rose and Andy, Death didn't have a punctuality problem.

"Promise me it won't hurt." Still, she couldn't look up at him. "The last time a heart attack nearly killed me, it hurt like hell."

"I can't…"

He didn't finish. Blythe went cold as she watched his loafers step toward her. This had to be it; her final moments on this earth. Not the worst place to go, she had to admit, in her favorite armchair. But it was a shame, *such* a shame, that Rose wasn't here to hold her hand. There was so much she wanted to tell her sweet, troubled daughter–her best friend–about life and love, about the secrets she'd never had a chance to share…

"I wish this didn't have to happen tonight," she admitted. "You know I'm not ready."

"Is that your family?"

Blythe glanced up at him, her gaze almost pleading. He was looking at the photo she'd stood next to her. The flicker of longing she perceived in his dark eyes had to be coming from her, she knew—hello, this was Death here—but it was all the hope she had left. That he might somehow take pity on her, gift her a bit more time so she could say goodbye to her children. She stared hard at him, projecting all her emotions.

"Those are my darlings, yes. They're all I have left in this world."

"What are their names?"

"Rose and Andy."

"Where are they?"

"Rose works in the city. She's promised to come and see me, though. She's supposed on her way tomorrow. If I could just have another day or two, I could—"

He interrupted with a slightly snappish "That isn't how things are done, you know."

Because everything he'd said beforehand had been so flat and emotionless, Blythe now sensed some sort of conflict in his voice. It took her aback, forced her to mentally reshuffle. She knew this was her shot— her only shot at convincing him.

"I realize it isn't strictly by the books, but I love my kids more than anything. All I'm asking for is a couple more days to say goodbye. After that, I swear I'll come gladly. Hell, when the time comes I'll even hurry *you* along."

He slowly paced to the sofa and back again without making a sound. Whatever was going on in his head, it had to be working in her favor, otherwise, he'd have shut her down straight away. Bizarrely, Death seemed to be in a quandary. She'd obviously got through to him somehow.

He sat facing her on the sofa, crossed his legs stiffly. "I accept your offer, Blythe."

"You do?" Resisting the urge to scream with relief, she replied, "Thank you. You don't know how much that means to me."

"You have three days from tomorrow."

"Three? That's more—I mean that's perfect. It's precisely what I would've chosen. Three days."

"With one condition," he added.

"Oh?"

"I will be your guest for those three days."

She squeezed one of her heart pills out of its foil wrapping and placed it under her tongue. "Okay, but what do you mean by a *guest*?"

"Call it what you will. Chaperon, escort, duenna. While you are here, I will be here."

"Actually, you're only a duenna if you're an older woman minding young girls. And Spanish."

He quirked an eyebrow. "Am I hearing things, or did you just correct me?"

Blythe took a nervous sip of water. "Sorry. Old habit. I used to teach history—that was before I *was* history."

"I know."

"How much do you know?"

"Enough."

"Then maybe you can tell me how I'm supposed to explain you to my visitors."

His turn to ruminate, but this time his silence didn't frighten her; it made her curious. The guy seemed so sure of himself, with that unearthly confidence, yet he didn't have an answer ready, as though this situation was a first for him, too. Then there was the Spanish word he'd gotten wrong. How could an omnipotent force of the universe possibly make a mistake like that? Come to think of it, why *was* he giving her this reprieve?

"If you don't mind me asking—and make no mistake, I'm eternally grateful and everything—but have you ever done this before? Granted a person extra time, I mean."

"Not exactly."

"So why me?"

"Why not you?"

Blythe pondered that one so hard that she pouted, something she'd done as a schoolgirl; and for the first time, Death smiled at her. It was a cute, cheeky lopsided grin that reminded her strongly of Hank Bonden, the boy's father when he'd been a similar age.

"Don't worry. That was a rhetorical question," he told her.

"Ah. Well, in that case, I'll repeat *my* question, which wasn't at all rhetorical. Why me?"

"Because you asked nicely."

"Yeesh. I wouldn't want to play *you* at poker. Or do you prefer chess?" She threw him a wink.

"Actually, I'm partial to Battleship." He returned the wink, and she didn't know whether to laugh out loud or shudder at the idea of the Grim Reaper having seen himself spoofed by an actor on screen. William Sadler, *Bill & Ted's Bogus Journey.* One of Rose's favorite films.

"So, who are you? I mean what are you? What do I call you?"

"Call me…Bellamy."

"Just Bellamy?"

"How about…Bellamy Scythe?"

Blythe pulled the two halves of her cardigan together and hugged herself. "Okay, just Bellamy." She shifted position, unsure of this new intimacy they were sharing. He still hadn't told her why he was doing this.

"The answers to all your questions will come in time," he said. "For now, think of me as an interested observer."

"Interested in what exactly?"

He brushed the knees of his trousers. "People, life, the things we take for granted."

"Wait a minute. You said *we*, not *you*. Why is that? Were you human at some point?"

"I was born, I lived, and I died."

"When was that?"

He grimaced. "A long time ago."

Blythe noticed the sun was still setting behind her; its glare continued to hold half the room in twilight. In fact, it hadn't faded in the slightest since Bellamy had appeared, as if he'd stopped time itself for this encounter.

"Interesting. Humor me, though. As I said, I used to teach history. So, which period are you from?"

His fingers wrought together in his lap. "I would prefer not to say. It's no longer important."

"Okay. But you do remember it, right? Your life?"

"In some ways."

"And this soul collecting thing is what—an indefinite assignment?"

He didn't reply. And that was all she could get out

of him regarding his nature and his past. Presumably, the Grim Reaper's contract of employment contained a nondisclosure clause. Either that or Bellamy just wasn't used to opening up. After all, therapists might be a little hard to come by in the Soul Creditors' Union.

But the longer they talked, well into the night, mostly about Blythe's teaching days and her family, especially her children, the more she missed Rose. Time for sleep was time wasted when she only had three days to play with. And chatting with Death while waiting to die was a tad…counter-productive.

"When do you expect her?" Bellamy asked as Blythe glanced at her favorite photo for the umpteenth time. This time, though, she picked up on an edge in his voice, a kind of enthusiasm. It struck her as strange, given his job, but she realized it had been there all along. But not all the time. No, it was whenever he spoke of Rose.

"Do I have to share everything?" she replied.

"Not everything."

"Then why so concerned?"

"As I said, I'm an interested—"

"Observer, yes. I got that part. If you must know, she'll probably be here shortly after breakfast. Rose doesn't do early unless it's fashionable to be late."

"Meaning what?"

"That she was born a rebel. Somebody in authority says jump, most people will ask how high. Rose, on the other hand, will make *them* jump for *her*."

He twitched a smile. "Did that disappoint you? To have a daughter turn out that way?"

"Are you kidding? It's my favorite thing about her. It makes Rose, well, *Rose*."

"Do you mind if I try it, then?"

"What? Telling her to jump?"

"Yes. It was amusing how you told it just now."

Blythe quirked an eyebrow. "Knock yourself out, pal. You might not be so amused when you get her reply."

"You sound defensive."

"You're the Grim Reaper."

His inscrutable gaze bore into her, as though he was trying to extract her thoughts about him. "Call me Bellamy."

"Okay, Bellamy," Blythe replied, enunciating every

syllable. "What if I told you I wanted to spend tomorrow alone with Rose?"

"Then you would be in error. I will be joining you tomorrow."

"Fair enough. But what if I told Rose not to come here at all? What if I don't want her to meet you? What would you say then, huh?"

"I would say our agreement is void. You asked for three days so you could spend time with your children. No children, no three days. Decide now, Blythe."

His poker face was something to behold, but there was that tension in his voice. An old emotion perhaps, bubbling to the surface.

"I was only asking," she said. "Of course, I'm going to see them, and you're welcome to tag along and…observe. So long as that's all you have in mind."

"Explain."

"I'd rather you didn't rub off on them. You know, the whole death thing."

"That isn't remotely what I had in—"

"Just so we know where we stand," she interrupted. "I'm grateful for the three days, I really am, but I would rather kill *myself* than to let you interfere with my kids' futures in any way. They are off-limits. Capiche?"

"You've made yourself clear, Blythe. Perhaps now we can be civil again."

"Fine by me. Perhaps now you'll let me rest for a while. We've got a big day tomorrow."

He ran a hand through his long hair with awe, as though enjoying the sensation of being inside a human body again, then laced his fingers on the back of his head, and watched her watching him. A million questions that had been flying around in her head suddenly settled and sank like damp leaves on a lake. Through his eyes, she saw herself clearly for the first time in a long time. The sum of everything she'd done. The things she still had left to do.

Best of all, she had tomorrow.

The rest would take care of itself.

"Will you be here all night, Bellamy, even if I fall asleep?"

"Perhaps."

"You don't have, you know, other appointments to keep?"

The sun finally disappeared, leaving the room in near-total darkness. He replied, "Do I have to share everything?"

CHAPTER TWO

The slow, deliberate rhythm of Rose's hiking boots creaking up the stairs to her mom's floor seemed to echo through the whole apartment building. It was that familiar weary self-consciousness that had followed her around for months now, ever since Mom's doctor had broken the bad news about her heart. Words like *degenerative, incurable,* and *lucky,* all used by Dr. Barkatali, were the toxic headlines from the worst day of her life. They framed her thoughts completely so that any time she wanted to feel good about spending time with her mom, they bled into her like black ink. Bad news ink; The heavy, poisonous kind that was hard to erase.

It was tough to stay upbeat when the blackness

began to run, and if Rose was honest, her demeanor was more Poison Oak than her namesake suggested even at the best of times. But more important than any of that—way more important than herself, for heaven's sake—she had to try to make her mom feel good today while stomping down the urge to cry. If her mother only had a matter of weeks, maybe even days left, then her last memories would not be of a sorry-for-herself, pissed-at-the-world daughter; they would be of her best pal, who was just glad to be with her.

She used her own key to let herself in. The smells of espresso and toast were strong, inviting.

"Hey, Mom," she called out just inside the door as she pulled down on the zipper of her leather bomber. "Any left in the pot for me?"

Hushed voices from the kitchen made her halt. She finished shedding her jacket in slow motion and felt for the switchblade in her jeans pocket.

"Warm day, huh? I thought we could take a walk, maybe feed the ducks or something," Rose spoke slowly, inching toward the kitchen, fully ready to stick anyone who made a wrong move against her.

She stepped into the kitchen, the toe of her boot gently pressing against the old black and white tile, blade un-drawn but at the ready. Her mom was leaning on the countertop, sipping coffee, her face flush, almost cheeky.

"Hi, sweetheart. I didn't expect you so early." That she didn't immediately introduce the young man sitting at the table spun all sorts of theories in Rose's mind, and none of them added up.

"And you are?" Rose asked him pointedly.

"Bellamy," her mom answered. "This is Bellamy. He's, ah, going to be with us for a day or two…visiting."

"Oh?" Rose quipped.

The man stood and bowed, not quite smiling, not quite anything, really. He was as blank as an inkless printout. Cute, though, in a lost, gormless kind of way; but she couldn't read him, and she couldn't profile him, both things that Rose was ordinarily very good at; first impressions were important in one of her two jobs, as an associate private investigator.

But damn it if she hadn't seen the guy someplace before. He was clean-shaven, long-haired and blonde, and dressed like a dork ready for Sunday lunch at the farmer's market. That knitted sweater, those loafers.

Yeesh.

"Pleased to meet you, Rose," he said.

The voice didn't ring any bells; maybe he just seemed familiar because he was the type she'd have gone for when she was in high school, without the dorky wardrobe, of course. Texan accent, too. Cute.

"Hey," she replied, and then to her mom, "Am I missing something? Since when did you have young gentleman callers?"

"It's, ah, kind of an important matter. I'd rather not go into all the details."

Her mom's cheeky, almost haughty air reminded Rose of herself as a girl, but far less abrasive. Yes, Rose had been a testy little shit, whereas her mother had been far more patient with her than she deserved. With Andy, too. Hell, *especially* with Andy. This was an interesting reversal.

Rose's first impulse told her it was a financial matter. This Bellamy character could be an accountant of some kind, advising her mom on what to do with her not-inconsiderable assets. Her divorce settlement had made her quite rich. Exactly *how* rich, Rose and Andy had only ever speculated on, and a topic that had become just too painful a topic for discussion lately, despite Andy's persistent callous probing.

"What firm are you with?" Rose asked the mystery visitor.

"I am a …an independent consultant," the guy replied with a stiff, yet eager, smile.

"What sort of consultant?"

"The kind that honors a client's confidentiality." He looked across to Blythe, who gave him a curt nod, then back to Rose. "It's at your mother's discretion, of course. But I think it's safe to say that my being here is to your benefit as well as Blythe's."

Crafty, enigmatic words that made her want to hack the truth out of him with an ice pick. God, how she hated bureaucrats and their legalese. It made her PI work ten times harder than it should be. But her mom wanted the creep here—that was that. She'd just have to wheedle the truth out of them some other way.

And Rose definitely had ways.

"Whatever," she said, waving his nonsense off. "So, Mom, how about that walk? If you've got any crusts saved up, we could feed the ducks."

Her mom's haughtiness dropped instantly, and she beamed. "Oh, I'd love that. Just let me get changed." On her way into the next room, she glanced at Bellamy from the corner of her eye. "Will you be alright waiting here? We won't be long."

"Where is it you're going?"

Blythe re-entered the room with a sweater wrapped around her. "To the park, just a few minutes away. There's a big pond where we sit and throw bread for the ducks. It's one of our favorite places." Rose liked her mother's emphasis on the word *our*. Just in case this bozo had the temerity to want to tag along.

"That sounds pleasant," he said. "I think I would like that."

"Oh, you *would*, would you?" Rose stepped between her mom and the shark. "Not to be a bitch or anything, but I didn't come here to see you, pal. I came for my mom. That's me and her. Two." She held up as many fingers to illustrate, then rudely widened them at him. "And you're what's in between. Clear enough?"

"Rose! There's no need for that."

A touch of anger, but a stronger dose of embarrassment marked her mom's words; neither fit her, because Blythe Foley was one of the most chilled and worldly women Rose had ever known. Nothing fazed her. So what had happened? Who *was* this Bellamy character?

"He's our guest," she went on, "not some snark target in one of your articles." The latter referenced Rose's primary job, as a freelance columnist for several women's magazines. "You need to show him some respect, because he's been good to me, and he *is* coming with us."

Rose mentally back-stepped, found she had no handle on this situation whatsoever. Was her mom taking this guy's side and dissing *her*? Any other time and she might have stormed out, but time was running out for her to say everything she wanted to say to her mom. From now on, *any* time they spent together was precious time, and if her mom wanted this jerk to be there with them, then it must be important. He must be important.

She promised herself she'd investigate the hell out of him the first chance she got. But for now…

"You're right, Mom. Sorry about that, Bernard." She shrugged dramatically. "I guess I misunderstood."

"It's Bellamy," he corrected her with an annoying grin.

"Yeah, that's what I said." Rose fished a fresh orange from the fruit bowl and started to peel it. "So, what's everyone standing around for? Are we going or what?"

Bellamy stared at her like she'd just beamed down from Planet Inappropriate. Her mother rolled her eyes, probably thinking how true that was.

"Yes, of course," she said, looking at Rose's jacket draped over the chair. "Is it cool out?"

"Nah, it's fine. Just grab a sweater for the waterfront. It gets windy down there."

Rose then straightened her black crop top with the *Punisher* logo in the center. She noticed Bellamy couldn't take his eyes off her, even when she met his gaze. It made her feel unusually uncomfortable, self-conscious, but she couldn't explain why. Guys checked her out all the time and made no effort to hide the fact; they were easy enough to brush off or flat-out ignore. But with this guy, there seemed to be no irony. No mental wink, nothing between his gaze and hers. It made her want to cover up, especially her bare midriff.

"Souvenir snapshots are available in the gift shop," she told him, clicking her fingers to break his gaze. "Hello. Earth to Bentley."

"Bellamy."

"Uh-huh. Like to look 'em right in the eye, don't you? Jeez."

"Excuse me?"

"Never mind. Something tells me you clean up at poker, that's all."

He cocked his head slightly to one side, and gently ran a hand through his long blonde hair, as though copying something he'd seen on a shampoo commercial. It was strange, the way he moved. A little awkward, and more than a little cute.

"Your mother said something very similar."

"What? About your poker stare?" Rose asked.

"Yes."

Rose stole a glance at her mom. "She should know. She cleans me out whenever we play."

"I think I would like to try that," Bellamy replied

cheerily.

"Cleaning me out? You might wanna hit the brakes there, Bub. We've only just met." Rose meant it as a snarky jab, but couldn't help but give the guy a warm grin.

He returned it, but only seemed to smile because she did. Rose suspected he hadn't understood a word she'd said. They spoke the same language, but then again, so had Chaucer and 50 Cent.

"You'll have to excuse my small talk," she told him. "I write snark for a living. It's hard to shake it sometimes."

"Snark?" Every letter came out as a question.

"Yeah. You know, snide remarks. Sarcasm. I snark at people who I think are asking for it. For blogs and stuff. People on the internet eat it up."

"I see. And…am I *asking* for it?" He seemed so unsure of the words he spoke.

"I haven't decided. Something's telling me it might be lost on you, Benjamin."

"Bellamy."

"That's what I said." She flicked him a wink. He returned it. Again, the awkwardness hung around.

The guy just flat-out had no guile, no social skills, or no social skills that she was used to, anyway. "Where exactly are you from?" she asked.

"Texas."

"Where in Texas?"

"El Paso. But I spent some time in England, in case you're wondering why my manners don't quite...what's the word...jive?"

"Ah, that explains it. Kind of." But it didn't. Not remotely. Rose had met plenty of Brits, and they were neither awkward to be around nor out of touch with the way Americans spoke. It was as if this guy came from a Texas of another age or a Great Britain of another time, altogether. She had to admit...she was intrigued. And more than a little puzzled about what he was doing here with her mom.

***

The three of them hardly spoke until they reached the park's ice cream vendor just past the skateboarding area, where Blythe licked her lips at the sight of a double scoop of strawberry and rum-raisin in a cone.

"Rose? Bellamy? Don't tell me you're not tempted."

"Try and stop me," replied Rose. Her mother always loved this ice cream stand. "You know what I like."

"Of course." Blythe turned back to the counter but glanced over her shoulder. "Bellamy?"

"Yes, please."

"What flavors do you want?"

He peered at the selection with his hands clasped behind his back, then shrugged. "I'll have whatever Rose is having."

"Living life on the edge?" Rose dampened down the sarcasm, remembering it was lost on him, but he was such an easy target.

The ice cream began to melt fairly quickly in the sun and Bellamy was like a little kid as he rushed to lick each and every drop of mint choc chip before it ran down the wafer to his fingers. Blythe chuckled as she watched him. Even Rose, who didn't know what to make of this persistent fish-out-water act, had to admit he *seemed* genuine. Enough to be disarming, at least. But her PI curiosity wasn't about to sit on the sidelines while he charmed her mom at this crucial time of her illness.

"So, how did you two first get in touch?" she asked. It was time to get to the bottom of this liaison.

"Your mother wanted a review of her affairs," replied Bellamy. "I was uniquely positioned to grant her request."

Rose quirked an eyebrow. "What does uniquely positioned mean?"

"Now, now," interrupted Blythe. "Let's leave the interrogation for another time. Try to switch off the Agatha Christie, just this once, okay, sweetheart?"

In frustration, Rose bit off an unladylike mouthful of ice cream and lobbed the remainder into the trash. It gave her brain freeze, and she had to squeeze her temples to ride out the discomfort. On to the duck pond, they strode. The grassy area surrounding the water was packed with picnickers and sunbathers and dog-walkers, who had to keep their pets leashed; too many dogs had jumped in after the ducks, and the authorities had put signs up all around the enclosure. Yeah, like that had ever worked. Rose counted three dogs paddling in the shallow areas and another, a black Lab, swimming after a stick in the middle of the pond.

Blythe picked a spot over near the reeds and the old, discolored fountain feature that still spat a trickle of water. The ducks were more sheltered here, and they flocked in when the first chunk of bread crust rippled the surface.

For once, Bellamy didn't seem bemused or out of his element as he distributed his crusts with perfect precision, landing them exactly in the path of each new bird, and making sure the same few greedy alphas didn't hog the feast.

"When was the last time you did this?" Rose asked him.

"A long time ago—at least, that's what it seems like."

"In England?"

"I don't remember. It was…"

"A long time ago. Yeah, I got that part. You seem to like it. I take it you're more into feeding ducks than shooting them?" He pinched his brow together and she held her hands up. "Just an impression."

"I wouldn't want to kill anything for sport," he replied. "I don't understand why a civilized person would want to end life purely for amusement."

"Unusual, coming from a Texan. And you spent time in Britain? I hear their Royals like to hunt things for fun."

Bellamy narrowed his eyes out across the water. "They should set a better example."

"Agreed. But we do seem fascinated by killing. As a species, I mean. I wrote this article a while back, about the relationship between pet owners and gun violence, and—"

"Maybe we should change the subject," Blythe cut in. "I think maybe death and killing aren't really the note we want to be striking. Not right now."

He flicked his eyes in Blythe's direction but remained quiet.

"Sheesh. You're right. Sorry, Mom. I just get carried away with—"

"It's alright, sweetheart. I tell you what, why don't we talk about what we're going to do over the next few days. Maybe map out an itinerary: favorite places, favorite eateries, *new* places, *new* eateries. I really want to enjoy it if I can."

"Sounds good to me," replied Rose, lowering her

voice when Bellamy got up to fish the Labrador's stick out of a bush thicket it was struggling with.

"Will, um, Belmont be joining us?"

Her mother rolled her eyes. "Yes."

She hadn't expected that answer. "What? *Everywhere?*"

Blythe nodded. "It's up to him, of course. But I've told him he's welcome to tag along whenever he wants."

"Yeah? That's…disappointing." Rose lobbed her final chunk of bread into the middle of the flock, sparking a free-for-all. "I was kinda hoping we could spend some time together. *Alone.*"

Her mom pondered that for a while, then said, "Sweetheart, there's something you should know. I probably wouldn't be here at all if it wasn't for him."

"What do you mean? Mom, why won't you tell me what's really going on between you two?"

"I will. I promise. In time."

"Well, you picked the wrong daughter to keep secrets from. I've got skills, you know."

Blythe grinned madly. "Oh yeah? So have I, Slick."

"I'm going to get to the truth if I have to shoot the

two of you up with Sodium Pentothal."

Blythe's mouth turned up in a mysterious smile, then she offered her hand. "I just need you to trust me, okay? Only for the next few days."

Rose took her mother's hand, kissed it. "I do. I will." She lowered her voice intentionally. "But I still think we should ditch the dork."

CHAPTER THREE

Rose pulled her phone from her back pocket and hastily typed a text message to her brother, Andy, both to ask when he was coming and to give him the heads up on this mysterious new interloper, but deleted it unsent at the last second. Call it intuition. Andy was whip-smart, but he was also confrontational; girls had always drooled over him, and his natural confidence had spun that adoration into something dangerously close to pomposity.

He said the first thing that popped into his mind, which, if you weren't feeding his ego, was often curt and cutting. Being without a father for many years hadn't helped the two of them growing up, but it had affected them in fundamentally different ways, Rose reckoned. She was a loner, whereas Andy craved attention. She loved her mom unconditionally, while Andy loved to be indulged by her.

It had set brother and sister at odds more times than Rose cared to remember, but there was always that unspoken, almost ironic alliance they shared, that seemingly nothing could break, not even when they came to fights. Fights which Rose had invariably won, having taken self-defense and karate classes since she was seven. It swayed her now.

She knew Andy so well, could almost predict what he'd say and do when he found out some stranger had their mom's ear at this late stage of her illness. The inevitable quarrel might even finish their mother off. No, it was better to keep her brother away until she could get a handle on what this Bellamy character was up to.

"Where to next?" he asked, brushing the dirt and breadcrumbs off his hands. "I saw some kids riding horses along a path, over that way." He pointed to the forest paths. "Are there horses for hire anywhere close by? I haven't ridden since...I can't remember when.

But it used to be…" Bellamy averted his gaze away from Rose, "one of my favorite things."

"Spoken like a true Texan." Rose watched for a reaction. He simply nodded, seemed lost in thought.

"Well, I wasn't planning anything so strenuous," replied Blythe. "But if you two want to go riding, there's no way I'm passing up the chance. *Let's saddle up!*"

"Mom? I didn't know you rode," Rose said, leery of this idea.

"Of course I can ride. It's just been a while, same as Bellamy."

"But…do you think it's wise?"

"You show me a wise man and I'll show you someone who never did anything worth a damn."

"Mom!" Rose couldn't help but laugh—seeing Blythe in this kind of form was the last thing she'd expected, and it was a glorious thing to behold. Almost out of time, she was turning back the clock. "What's gotten into you?"

"I don't know. I feel like going on an adventure."

Blythe took both Rose and Bellamy by the arm and led them toward the stables with the spring in her step it didn't seem half that far. On the way, they stopped and each had a turn at a little shooting gallery hut in the park's central square. Bellamy won a great big fluffy bear, which he then gave to Rose. She thanked him, but in turn, gave it to a little girl who was crying in a stroller nearby. The girl's eyes lit up, her tears stopped, and she held the bear tightly.

"Okay, now it's my turn to ask. What's gotten into *you*?" Blythe gave Rose's arm a gentle squeeze as they waved goodbye to the girl and her parents. "That was really sweet."

"I'm not five anymore, Mom," she replied.

Bellamy gave Rose another one of his inscrutable, questioning looks that deflated her a little. Why was he always looking at her?

"I've not offended you, have I?" she asked, in a mocking tone to poke at their guest.

"No…and yes."

"She didn't mean it that way," Blythe cut in. "She just paid your kindness forward. Maybe where you come from, there's a different—"

"No need to explain."

Rose held up her hands in a mock apology. "Sorry. I

guess I should've asked you first."

Bellamy said nothing. Instead, he gave an odd, lopsided smile that was somehow lost in translation. Rose took her mom by the arm and led them to the stables, but it seemed to take an inordinately long time to get there. Blythe kept stopping, looking around, then slowing to catch her reflection in a window or the reflection of something behind her. Bellamy noticed it, too, but he didn't seem fazed by it, didn't even bother to see what she was looking at.

"Everything okay?" asked Rose.

Blythe replied, "Fine," and paid for the hire of three horses for up to two hours. It wasn't until they reached the old, overgrown baseball diamond, about a twenty minutes' trot from the stables, that Blythe started glancing behind her again, now to either side, constantly scanning the trees and the paths for…whatever it was. She suddenly retrieved her Smartphone from her shoulder bag and held it out at her side for several seconds.

Rose had had enough. She made her horse gallop ahead until she was side by side with her mom. "What's the deal? You were filming something just now. What was it?"

"I thought you were supposed to be the observant one."

"Um, yeah, I just observed you."

Blythe rolled her eyes. "Take a look at this, Sherlock," she said, handing Rose the phone, "and tell me you haven't seen this guy at least a dozen times since we left the house."

The man riding a bicycle in the footage was dressed like a golfer; pastel green polo shirt, beige trousers, white shoes, sunglasses. And no, she had to admit that she hadn't spotted him once. "You think he's been following us?"

"I *know* he's been following us. On foot at first. He didn't appear on a bike until we were on horseback, must have rented one from the bike shop next to the stables."

"You're certain?"

"Adamant."

"Okay, so now we have to find out which one of us he's following, and why."

"How do we do that?" asked Blythe.

"Leave that to me." Rose's stock reply when she had

no clue how to proceed in a private investigation or a story for her column. Projecting confidence was important in every situation in a big city, she'd come to learn if a woman wanted to be taken seriously. Now it was a habit.

The guy was still there, peddling along the track parallel to the bridle path, at a discreet enough distance behind them but nonetheless exactly where she would be if she were shadowing a mark. This had to be about Bellamy. The timing was just too striking. His sudden appearance, unknown background, his mysterious assignment, her mom being so defensive about him; it all pointed to something unsavory.

She slowed down, waited for Bellamy to catch up. "Ever seen that man before?" She pointed out the solitary cyclist, and he must have seen her because he suddenly sped up and peddled out of sight.

"No." Bellamy seemed unsure.

Rose didn't buy it. "Any reason you might be followed?"

"None that can think of."

Rose clucked her tongue as she eyed him. "Just a leaf in a breeze, huh?"

He quirked a grin and met her stare. "If you like."

Rose jabbed a threatening finger at him. "If I find out you're lying, you'll find out how fast that breeze becomes a freakin' hurricane. Okay?"

He shrugged in reply, then motioned to a row of hedges ahead to their left. There was a long field beyond it, with soccer posts lying flat on the grass and a large, deflated bouncy cushion and some kind of generator with a fan inside. Bellamy dug his heels into his horse's sides and geed it into a sprint. Rose watched in awe as Bellamy made his way ahead of them.

He cleared the hedge, circled the field, and jumped back onto the path they were on, drawing applause from passersby. "I didn't spot the fellow," he reported. No doubt the guy could ride, and shoot, and be sweet and polite. But right now, he was between Rose and the truth.

Not a place he would stay for very long.

The mystery cyclist never showed up again for the remainder of the day, not even after they brought the horses back, but Rose was constantly on her guard, watching for loiterers or loners or anyone casting a curious eye in her mom's direction, or Bellamy's. The latter did draw quite a lot of attention, mostly of the admiring female kind, everyone from college-age girls to middle-aged women checking him out in often not-so-subtle ways. Not that surprising really; his unusual blend of bad boy biker looks and almost wistfully naïve tourist demeanor made him stand out. Made him interesting; a genuine conundrum in a world of petty absolutes.

And to the guy's credit, he didn't let the attention go to his head in the slightest, or if he did, he didn't show it. Instead, he strolled alongside Rose and Blythe with a kind of carefree, amused curiosity, as though it was all a dream and he was the only one who knew it. Nothing bad could happen to him in this dream, therefore everything was inconsequential. Rose knew that if she hadn't grown so cynical, so paranoid, thanks in no small part to her part-time PI work, she would probably find Bellamy appealing, maybe even charming. She found herself watching his lips as he spoke about his love of riding again.

"A manicured bridle path can't compete with the wild Devonshire beaches," he lamented. "I used to spend summers with my cousins at Mere Hall, my uncle's country estate—he'd bought himself a baronetcy—" He stopped dead, as though he'd said too much, then added, "I mean he was good enough to let us ride his Spanish mares up and down the beach to our hearts' content. I don't remember much about my life in England, but I'll never forget sprinting through the surf in those driving Devonshire winds, feeling like the mares could sprout wings and take off at any moment, like a herd of Pegasus."

"Ooh, Pegasus—I saw that movie!" Rose butted in, immediately wishing she hadn't. Listening to Bellamy wax poetic was like traveling back in time somehow, to an era before snark. The way he phrased his words, it wasn't exactly Vogue speak. "Um, Harryhausen, right?"

"That's the one," he replied, a look of awe washed over his face. "Amazing what he did before CGI."

Now they were talking about something Rose loved. Movies. "I know, right? Kids nowadays take it all for granted, all the computer effects. I think it's taken the make-believe out of the magic. But Harryhausen, man, he gave those creatures personality. They might be a bit jerky, but you could tell they were actually *there,* physically. They were real, in a sense."

It appeared that Bellamy shared a similar affection. "Exactly. Those skeletons in *Jason and the Argonauts,*" he replied with enthusiasm, "it actually made them seem more real *because* they were slightly jerky, rickety somehow like you'd imagine reanimated skeletons to be. Like you say, it's the make-believe, that slight element of unreality, that leaves a lasting impression on the viewer."

"You're a guy after my own heart, Bertrand," replied Rose. "Isn't he, Mom? I've been saying those exact same things for years."

But her mom nodded with pursed lips. "Hmm."

Was is something Rose had said?

"Mom? You with us?"

"Uh-huh. Jason and the Argonauts. Skeletons. You're full of surprises, aren't you, *Bellamy.*"

The sudden sharpening of her voice on his name turned the words into a stern rebuke, the kind she might have given to one of her testy students. It flipped not only the conversation but the entire outing, on its head. Rose felt a little bad for him at first—the poor guy was only making friendly chit-chat—but now she realized his relationship with her mom was not as easygoing as the two of them had tried to make out.

"Okay, Mom, this is getting weird," she spoke. "You brought him with us, you clearly wanted us to get along and, yet, the first time we *do* get along you snap at him for it? Care to explain what's really going on here?"

Blythe heaved a big sigh, composed herself, then shrugged. "It's nothing. I was distracted, is all."

Rose whipped her head to their guest. "Bellamy?"

He just gave her an innocent shrug as he noticed a drip of ice cream on his shirt and began wiping at it.

"Then either you're both hiding something or I need an antipsychotic."

"Perhaps you'd settle for another ice cream?" suggested Bellamy, tucking his long hair back behind his ears. "I do fancy myself some more of that mint chocolate chip flavor."

Rose threw her hands in the air. "Oh, by all means."

He sprouted one of his sweet, unassuming smiles,

then made a beeline for the ice cream stand, even jockeyed for position in the line when a young boy wearing an Avengers sweatshirt tried to hustle ahead of him. Rose rolled her eyes as she watched the two of them semi-playfully shove each other, and decided to settle it herself.

Standing tall over the boy, she pointed to the Punisher logo on her T-shirt, a white skull-mask on a black background, and the boy awkwardly stepped away while muttering a profanity far too mature for his innocent lips. Rose, triumphant, grinned and looked to Bellamy; his careless gaze fixated on her shirt. He seemed troubled and curious at the same time; the gloss over his distant eyes reflecting something hidden deep inside. Something Rose was determined to uncover.

She snapped her fingers in front of his nose. "Hey, buddy, I'm up *here.*"

His handsome, but blank face seemed to reanimate and an answering smile spread across it. He adjusted his stance and stood straight. "Apologies. I…seem to have drifted off in thought."

Rose rolled her eyes. "Whatever. The kid is gone.

We getting' ice cream, or what?"

The fog of his daydream still seeming to linger, Bellamy nodded quickly and stepped forward in line. "Oh, yes, of course. The young man. Quite unruly, isn't he?"

"I take it you don't have kids, either?"

He slanted her an ironic glance—the first she'd seen him give. The piercing of his eyes caused an unexpected thump in her chest. "What was your first clue?"

"Uh, call it a hunch." Rose willed her heart to slow and the flush to recede from her cheeks. What was wrong with her? She shook her head and, after making sure her mom wasn't standing next to them, she leaned in and said, "Just between us, is she in any trouble?"

He didn't answer straight away, and Rose was about to repeat the question when he shook his head. "We have an arrangement," he said. "I'm afraid it's between us."

"It's starting to sound illegal."

"It isn't," he insisted politely.

She chewed at her lip. "And I'm supposed to just

take your word for that?"

"No. You should take your mother's."

"Really? What's your surname then?"

Annoyance seemed to be building in his solid demeanor, but he didn't act on it. He muttered something that sounded like *scythe*. Rose cupped her hand to her ear, tilted it toward him.

"Come again?"

"Smith. Bellamy Smith," he quickly repeated.

"That's your real name?"

He hesitated. "Yes."

They stared at one another for a long moment.

"I'm onto you, pal. I'm watching your every move."

Not only did he *not* take that as a threat, the guy even seemed to like the idea. Umpteen times she caught a twitch of a smile on his lips as he gazed back at her. And Rose found herself slipping into a bizarre quandary, one she couldn't reconcile on any level. Everything about his relationship with her mom told Rose that he was up to no good, that he couldn't, *shouldn't* be trusted. But even face to face and at close quarters, she had a hard time detecting any deceit in him.

More than that, and against her every twenty-first-century impulse, as much as she hated to admit it, Rose found herself wanting to believe him. Maybe it was his politeness or his stunningly good looks. Or that he seemed a little lost, a long way from home. Or it might have been the Harryhausen touch—the way he'd described make-believe.

There was something not quite real about him, that was for sure. And true to her promise, she watched his every move. It wasn't difficult.

She couldn't take her eyes off him.

CHAPTER FOUR

After their morning with the horses and indulging in ice cream, it was time for some real food. A group of street musicians bellowed tuneful classics from the lawn in front of the café where Blythe and Rose were eating lunch and a small crowd had gathered outside the doors to listen to the musicians.

The temperature continued to climb, and by two-thirty the park was bustling. Bellamy, munching on his second bacon cheeseburger, stood apart from the crowd, alone atop a grass verge, lost in the music and the all-around upbeat atmosphere of the park. It was the first time he'd left Blythe's side since Rose had arrived, and though Rose was dying to quiz her mom about him, she didn't want to pressure her unduly. For one thing, her mother's color was not good—ashen, in fact, and there was that horrible shortness of breath that could easily be a precursor to a heart attack. The final heart attack.

"What if we switch tables—get further inside—cool you off in front of the AC?" Rose spotted an empty table near the fake potted palm tree whose fronds were fidgeting in the stream of cool air.

Blythe wiped her brow with her handkerchief, cast a slightly worried glance at Bellamy outside, then nodded to Rose. "Just till I cool off."

She could walk fine on her own, but Rose wasn't taking any chances. She held her mom's arm while they crossed the busy café, then went back to fetch their drinks. "Have you taken any of your heart pills today?"

"Way ahead of you, sweetie." Placing a tiny white dot under her tongue—a tablet so small it probably wouldn't even ripple the water next to the crumbs if it fell in the duck pond, yet for Blythe, it was the difference between life and death. Yes, her existence was *that* fragile right now.

The idea took Rose's breath away.

"Ah, that's better." Blythe held her face up in the steady air stream, closed her eyes. "So, what's new in the city, Rosie?"

"Not a lot. Thicker air, thinner hair, caffeine keeping the whole place awake. Same old, same old."

Her mom chuckled, still with her eyes closed. "So young to be so jaded. What do you do for fun?"

"Fun? I actually heard a rumor that someone somewhere had some fun once."

"What happened?"

"They got arrested."

Blythe playfully shook her head. "Poor Rosie. It's like I keep telling you, when your glass is half-empty, don't hold onto it, pour it out and order something new." She waggled her eyebrows. "Preferably something stronger."

"Mom, I always knew you were a lush," Rose kidded.

"Of course. It gets me through the day." Blythe gave a laugh.

Rose grinned and crossed her arms over her chest as she leaned back in her chair. "You're bad."

"Yup, and I have the pills to prove it." Blythe rubbed her eyes before opening them. "Seriously, though, sweetie, you need to take my advice and make more time for yourself. You're working way too hard. When was the last time you called a guy up when he gave you his number?"

"Let me see… Yeah, that new lawyer I hired."

"Is he cute?"

"God no. He looks like Gollum. But he's as smart as they come."

"Okay, when was the last time you went out on a date?"

"Mom, stop."

"Why? I know you have tons of offers."

"Yeah, well, so does eBay."

In between sips of her iced tea, Blythe rolled her eyes. "I was like you for a while before college. I didn't want to get stuck with one of the guys from my home town just because they were there, because of a lack of options; it made no sense to me. Geography determining one's future? I hated that idea. So, I left as soon as I could to see what else was out there."

"And you met Dad in college, and never lived in

your home town again. So, you were right all along. You were right not to settle for those limited options. You went out and found new ones. Which is exactly what I've been saying. Dating should be an adventure; it should be about wanting to take risks. But like you said, *I* have to be the one doing the choosing. I'm not going to let geography determine who I end up with."

"You didn't let me finish." Blythe solemnly traced her finger around the rim of her glass. "There's a part I left out, a part I've never told you before."

Rose tilted her head slightly to one side and leaned forward then, ready to listen closely.

"It's about what really happened in college," her mom went on. "I think it's something you should know…before…it might explain…" She glanced outside to where Bellamy now appeared to be awkwardly mingling with the crowd a little.

"Explain what?"

"It might help to clarify…a number of things that have happened."

"Like what?" Rose looked outside again, scrutinizing their mysterious chaperone. "Who is he, Mom? Who is he really? I swear I've seen him before, but I can't place him."

A long, weary sigh that Rose could tell contained all the answers to her questions, brought Blythe back to her story. She either would not, or could not, betray Bellamy yet. And the more she dodged the question, the deeper the hole she was digging for him, and for herself.

"You know your dad and I met in our sophomore year, at a beat poetry night, right?"

"Uh-huh. Some Bohemian dive with no windows. I remember the story."

Blythe shook her head in amusement. "Only the worst poetry and even worse pot, all you could smoke of either. Your dad wrote what I called 'beat-up' poetry, the kind you could only possibly come up with after you'd just suffered several hard knocks to the head."

"Oh, I know the type." Rose recalled some of the awful poetry joints around the city where she lived. Sometimes a freelance job would force her to suffer through it for the sake of a written review. Roses words were never kind to the poets.

"Yeah, well at least he had some clue of how bad he

was. The ironic applause coming from my table might have stung a, shall we say, more precious poet, but your dad was in on the joke. He laughed when I asked if he'd just made it up on the fly; he said that kind of thing was impossible. I said it wasn't just possible, it was the essence of beat poetry. So, he challenged me and the guy I was with to improvise something on stage."

"The guy you were with? You mean you were dating someone else when you met Dad?"

"We'd been going steady since freshman year."

"Who was he? You've never mentioned him."

"Turned out he knew your dad from way back, from high school. They'd been pals, but hadn't kept in touch."

Rose sat up. "So, Dad stole you from this guy?"

"That's the part I'm getting to." Again, she checked over her shoulder, making sure Bellamy was still out of earshot. "Anyway, we killed it on stage, me and Hank—that was his name—Hank Bonden—with a kind of demented, pot-fueled stream-of-consciousness double-act that only made sense if everyone else was high as a kite. And they were. We titled it *Pots for Rags.* To this day I don't know how we did it, but it was the best performance of the night, and it got us free drinks."

Blythe stopped to take a long sip of her iced tea.

"Hank and your dad kinda picked up where they left off at first, but things quickly became tense between them, because your dad couldn't stop himself from hitting on me. Not just flirting; he was trying to feel me up right there at the table in front of Hank. It seemed funny at the time, as most things do when you're stoned, but later on, I realized how stupid I'd been. I didn't hit the brakes; I didn't tell your dad enough was enough. No, Hank had to do that. He stepped in and put a stop to it. He shoved your dad away. And when your dad swung a punch and missed, Hank threw him across the room. To cut a long story short, we all got arrested, and things were never the same between me and Hank."

"Holy crap! So, Dad really did split you up. What a prick. Did you ever see this Hank guy again?"

"On and off throughout college. We stopped speaking altogether, though, when he found out I'd started dating your dad."

"Not behind his back?"

"No, no. I was a lot of things, but I never cheated on any guy I was with. Of course, Hank didn't see it that way. He said I'd encouraged your dad that night at the poetry...what do you call them nowadays...slam?"

"Kind of. But did you?"

"Did I what?"

"Encourage him that night?"

Behind Blythe's carefully modulated expressions, a touch of regret twitched her impressively wrinkle-free skin here and there, especially around the eyes. She might be telling the truth, but it was nonetheless only a version of it, one she'd edited long ago for her own peace of mind. Being completely honest after all this time was probably impossible. She was seeing that pot-fueled night through forty years of hedging and revising and second-guessing.

"I didn't say no," she admitted. "And I could have. I *really should* have."

"All this time and you're still cut up about it? How serious *was* this Hank?"

Blythe paused to consider and didn't bother wiping

the dampness from her eyes. "The love of my life."

Rose said nothing while her mom fought back the urge to weep. Somewhere inside her deep surprise at this confession, a few inklings of even deeper understanding began to flash. Things Rose had never tried to make sense of before, but which, in this new context, absolutely did make sense. About her mom. About her dad. About that day at the fair when she'd been twelve. It suddenly sprang to mind. Dad's friend, but Dad not being there, how happy Mom had seemed, and how everything had changed—absolutely everything about their lives—after the fire.

"The fire," Rose spoke out loud. "He was there that day, wasn't he? That was him. That was Hank."

Blythe wiped her eyes with heels of her palms, nodded quickly. "I wasn't sure if you remembered that or not."

"Only fragments. I know you never talked about it after, but I still remember bits and pieces, like the hot dog stand spilling over into the hay, and the hay catching fire…"

"What else?"

"Some kind of tent was burning, too. A red one.

Was it a big top?"

"There were two tents. Nothing so big, but there were people inside."

"And I remember a really loud bang, like a giant tire bursting."

"A car's tires," Blythe explained. "The fire spread around the parking lot."

"And screaming. I definitely remember screaming. From high up, I think?"

"There were people on the Ferris Wheel when it happened. The fire crew fought like crazy to keep the flames away from them. Luckily, *they* all survived. I can't imagine what that must have been like, trapped in midair like that, watching the flames growing higher, knowing there's nothing you can do…"

Strange and shocking, how the memories Rose had suppressed all these years—fifteen years or more— tumbled into her mind's eye like the shards of glassy rocks unearthed and collided by a sudden avalanche of associations. She hadn't lost anyone close to her that day, but people had died. And "Daddy's friend", as Mom had introduced the man who'd accompanied them that day, *had* lost someone. That much she did remember.

"There was a guy that got burned—I don't think he made it." Rose spun her sweaty Pepsi glass with her fingers, trying to summon some detail about the boy, anything that might spark a recollection. She drew a blank. "Hank's son, right?"

Blythe shifted uncomfortably in her seat, but it wasn't her heart this time; her color had mostly returned, and she didn't appear quite so out of breath. Tired, yes, but very much alert and in the conversation. "You have a good memory," she said. "You only met him that one time—the day he died."

"I don't remember anything about him, except…I think he sat next to me on one of the rides. It made me feel really grown up, and I wanted someone from school to see me with him. He was a lot older than me, right?"

"He was in his twenties. His name was Thomas."

"How did he die?"

"He was watching the magic show in one of the tents when it caught fire. The magician's assistant was a gorgeous redhead in a skimpy outfit, so naturally, Tom was on the front row. Apparently, he had a thing for redheads."

"Most guys do."

"It was what killed him. When the panic started, he was one of the farthest from the exit. The fire spread so quickly, he had no chance. One of the survivors said Tom made a last-ditch attempt to follow the magician and the assistant out through the backstage exit, but he'd left it too late. The tent roof collapsed, burying him in flames. He was burned alive."

"Jesus," Rose said in a hollow reply and downed the last of her Pepsi, "Abraca-freaking-dabra."

Her mom watched her carefully, appeared to be waiting for some sort of penny to drop. She didn't elaborate.

"Did the magician and the assistant make it out?"

"Yes. Only four people were killed altogether, which is pretty remarkable considering the size of the blaze and how many were there that day. Three died in that particular tent, and one in the next tent, before the firefighters showed up. Dozens were treated for severe burns. All in all, not a good day to be at the fair."

"So, let me get this straight. You and Hank reunited

at some point, years after college, and started seeing each other again before that day at the fair?" Blythe stayed silent, which was as good as an admission. "Did you and Dad split up *before* you got back with Hank?"

"Before it got serious, yes. But we had seen each other a few times before that, me and Hank. I'll not deny it. Those old feelings never went away."

"Behind Dad's back?" Rose tried her best to subdue the flash of anger she felt.

"Your dad and I were never all that close, Rosie," Blythe explained. "There was an attraction, and we always respected each other, but I don't think either of us was under any illusion that it was all it could be. When you've known the kind of love I had with Hank in college, you can't help but compare every other guy to him and the way he made you feel. So, there was that, which might not sound fair. But on the other hand, your dad wanted a career, a family, a fortune, a big house, an important legacy, like some kind of formula. I was just one more component he had fixed in his life plan, and it just wasn't enough for me."

She paused a moment to take in a deep breath.

"By the time we had you, he was spending more time at the office than he was at home, even on weekends. I put up with it for a while because I had you to keep me busy, and to be honest, I thought he might make more of an effort with a baby daughter to come home to. And he did, but not enough. His heart wasn't in it. Everyone could see that. Some people just aren't cut out to be parents. Men and women. It's not something you can know until you've tried it, I guess. And when we had Andy, well, the writing had been on the wall for a long time. Your dad had gotten his career, his fortune, his big house, his important legacy—he was brilliant at what he did— but he came to realize he'd lost his family somewhere along the way. Or rather, I pointed it out to him, perhaps in ways I'm not too proud of. But the fact is he was never the husband or the dad he needed to be, and I was in love with someone else."

A cold feeling ran through Rose's veins. "Why be so honest about it all of a sudden? You've never said any of this before now."

"Why be honest *now?*" Blythe quirked an eyebrow.

"Do I really need to answer that?" Leaning across the table, she squeezed her daughter's hand. "Let all the poisons that lurk in the mud hatch out."

"I, Claudius." Rose snorted a mirthless chuckle. "You always did read too much history, Mom."

"One can never read too much history, or learn enough from it."

"Uh, yes, Mrs. Foley." Rose always enjoyed poking fun at her mom for being such a great teacher.

"Little bugger."

Just as Rose was about to ask what happened between her mom and Hank, Bellamy breezed in, asking if he could have another glass of what Rose was drinking.

"Knock yourself out, bud." Rose pointed him to the self-service soda dispenser. When he shrugged, she rolled her eyes and leaped up impatiently, grabbing the empty glass. This beautiful dummy was like some lost time traveler inflicted on the twenty-first century—on Rose in particular. "Enjoy the band?" she asked sarcastically as she made her way over to the dispenser, Bellamy in tow.

"They were passable," he replied, caressing an ice

cube in his palm as though it was the neatest invention since flip flops. "But they could use some finesse."

"Let me guess, you were a composer in a past life."

"I played the piccolo," he replied matter-of-factly, not picking up on her sarcasm.

"Blew hard, too, I'm betting." When he missed it a second time, she rolled her eyes. "Sorry. I mean, I bet you were good," she lied and then handed him the soda.

His hand brushed against her fingers and time seem to slow around them, the background dulling, just for a brief moment. It was an odd sensation as if her ears had suddenly become full of water. But the shine in Bellamy's eyes told her he felt it, too. His gaze now drifted to her mouth and grazed over her parted lips. The invitation there, he began to lean in towards her, her ears ringing with heat and heart pounding against the inside wall of her chest as if it would reach out and grab Bellamy by the shirt collar to draw him closer. Faster.

But before she could wrap her mind around the flicker of a moment, her mother came up from behind. "Why don't we head back to the apartment? I'm sure poor Bellamy here's had enough of our boring outing."

He regained his stance but never removed his eyes from Rose's lips. "On the contrary, I've quite enjo–"

"Fine, humor me then. I'm old and tired. Bring me home." With a sudden impatience, Blythe grabbed his shoulder and led him back to the table.

Rose's mother glanced back and forcefully grinned at her, then commiserated Bellamy with a pat on the shoulder. Rose watched, still breathless, as her mom spoke into Bellamy's ear before grabbing her handbag. And just like that, Rose felt like an outsider in her own family. It was hard to explain. They'd been hush-hush about their liaison before, but now it was as though they'd thrown the gauntlet at her feet, *taunting* her with secrecy. If it was a tease before, it was an outright challenge now. A challenge for her to uncover the truth. If she could keep her hormones in check long enough.

Time to make a few calls.

CHAPTER FIVE

So much for the calls. Eddie Dobkin, her boss at Dobkin & Searle Investigations, was incommunicado and would be for the remainder of the afternoon.

"Someone *else* has filed a lawsuit against us," his secretary, Helen, explained. "Can you believe that? That's two in two weeks. He's called Mr. Searle back from Toronto, and they're both lawyering up in a hurry. If I were you, Rosie, I'd leave it 'till tomorrow, unless it's an emergency. You know what Eddie's like when he's up against it."

She sure did. Prickly was the kindest word she could

think of to describe him when things weren't going his way. "Gotcha. Is Marty there?"

"No. He skipped out quickly as soon as he saw Mr. Searle arrive."

"Nicky?"

"Her too."

"Jesus. What about Alex?"

"He's, ah, out on assignment, I think. Hasn't logged in since…let me see…" A sequence of rapid keystrokes later, "It's been a couple of days, at least. Must be deep cover."

Rose sighed, waved back to her mom who was signaling that they were ready to leave the café. "Okay, thanks, Helen."

"It's not an emergency, then? 'Cause if it is, you know, I can always go get—"

"No, that's okay. It's nothing I can't handle. No point getting your head bitten off by Unsteady Eddie. I'll figure something out."

"If you're sure…"

"Positive."

"Stay safe, Rosie."

"Later."

Her final call before returning to her mom was to Marty Brigman directly. It went straight to voicemail, so she decided to leave him a message. None of the associate investigators at Dobkin & Searle particularly liked her—they thought she was too brash and way too sarcastic, which was mostly true—but Marty at least tolerated her more than the others did. Except maybe Eddie Dobkin, who found her snark amusing when he wasn't bouncing off the walls.

"Hey, Marty, it's Rosie. Listen, I know I already owe you one—okay, about seven or eight—but I really need a favor. It affects my mom. You know she's sick, and the doctors say she hasn't got long left." Rose swallowed hard and tried not to look across the café towards her mom. "There's this guy with her, never leaves her side, someone I've never met before. He says he's some kind of freelance consultant. Mom won't tell me any more than that, and he won't break his client privilege. There's something not quite kosher about it—the timing, the secrecy, and he's really…weird." She shivered at the thought.

"Also, I'm almost positive someone is surveilling us. Pretty sure it's the new guy he's keeping tabs on, and not us. Mom doesn't *appear* to be in any distress, but I don't wanna take any chances. Anyway, if you could track down any information on a Bellamy Smith or Smythe from El Paso, that would be fantastic. He's mid-twenties, Caucasian, blonde, says he lived in the UK for a while when he was younger. Check out the relevant Texan registries—accountants, legal, criminal—whatever you can think of. I'd do it myself but I really don't want to leave the two of them alone. Please get back to me as soon as you get this message. There's a complimentary blow-job in it for you."

She threw the last bit in as a joke. Poor Marty had a crazy jealous wife and Rose loved to stir things up. It was more detailed than her usual curt messages, but she wanted to find out as much as possible before her brother Andy got there and threw a hissy fit like the man-child he was.

"Hey, sorry. Work stuff. Home?" she asked her mom and her mysterious chaperone; the two now walked arm-in-arm.

"Yes, I think that's enough for me for one day." As if sensing her daughter's unease, Blythe offered Rose her other arm, so the three of them left the park together. Out of the corner of her eye, Rose spotted the mysterious cyclist, who was now on foot. He kept a much more discreet distance, but he was still following them. That much she was sure. Rose said nothing but kept tabs on him. He followed them out of the park and for at least three more blocks, then she lost sight of the stalker.

***

Blythe said she'd had enough of TV, so they played Monopoly in her living room instead. Strangely, Bellamy had never played it before, though he did pick it up no time. He seemed to have *all* the luck as well, which irritated Rose to no end because he took delight in teasing her whenever she had to pay him. So, she cheated at every opportunity, helping herself and her mom stay in the game while undermining his almost supernatural dominance in property development.

Her mom knew what she was doing and had to cover her mouth to keep the chuckles in whenever she spotted one of Rose's sleights of hand. Bellamy, however, didn't pick up on it until one of his hotels mysteriously got downsized to a green house. When Rose landed on that property, his usual haughty gloat turned into the deepest, most bamboozled frown she'd ever seen. He gaped at his opponents, then slumped into a deadly serious re-examination of the board and everyone's holdings. The poor guy doubted his own sanity rather than entertain the notion that he'd just been punked.

It was beyond sweet and Rose thought he was painfully cute as he scrambled with his thoughts. And although she couldn't help blurting out a cackled laugh at his expense—exceeded only by her mom's infectious belly laugh—Rose actually felt bad when she finally owned up to cheating. It was like she'd let him down somehow and dirtied the rose-colored glasses through which he'd seemed to have seen until now. She was about to reach over and grab his hand to ensure a better apology but stopped when her phone buzzed against her leg in the pocket of her jeans.

"Hey, Marty." She stepped into the apartment building's hallway after surrendering her last pitiful holdings in the game and shut the door behind her. The signal wasn't great. His voice kept breaking up, so she asked him to hang on until she got down to the street for better cell reception. "Okay, try again. You still there?"

"Yeah. We'll have to make it quick, though," he replied. "My wife'll be here in a few minutes. I don't have to tell you what that means."

"Gotcha." Contrary to popular rumor, Rose had never seduced Marty or got him to do any of those hardcore things she hinted at now and then in office gossip. Something about her borderline goth-girl appearance and rebel attitude seemed to convince people that she was some sort of man-eating sexual deviant, which was so spectacularly off the mark that Rose had stopped denying it years ago. At least Marty knew the rumors weren't true. Unfortunately, his wife Jamie wasn't taking any chances. She hated Rose with a vengeance, by all accounts hated even the thought of her, whatever that meant.

"No trace of your guy, at least not in Texas. A handful of Bellamy Smiths, even a Bellamy Smythe, but all old-timers. None even close to matching your description. I checked all the relevant registries. Probably worth broadening the search, but not unless you're certain that's his real name."

"His accent is definitely Texan."

"Could be a fake."

"Possibly, but I doubt it."

"And you don't have any more specifics? His professional credentials would be a good place to start. We could easily track him down with those, provided he's given you his real name."

"Yeah, that's going to be tricky. Mom's tight-lipped about the whole thing. I could try to trick it out of them, but to be honest they're all over my crap. I don't know what else to do. No point contacting the police because Mom's adamant that everything's fine."

"Uh huh. But they'd be able to verify his ID and his credentials. If you told them you suspected he was there on false pretenses, they'd be obliged to investigate. That would clear everything up, or at least validate your suspicions. On the other hand, your mom…"

"Would hate me for not trusting her. And like I said, she doesn't have long left. Something like that could kill her—the stress of it.”

“She doesn’t seem under any kind of duress as things are?”

“Not really, no. She’s actually enjoying herself more than I’ve seen her in ages. It’s good to see.”

“Then I hate to say it, but maybe you *should* trust her. Maybe this guy is genuinely helping her.” Marty paused. “What does your gut tell you about him, Rose?”

“That he’s got too many secrets…” She glanced up at her mom’s window, but the oblique angle didn’t allow her to see anything more than the sunset’s dazzling reflection on the glass. “But also, that he’s not lying necessarily. It’s hard to explain. He seems like a sweet guy, but there’s a dark side—that’s where the secrets lie. I just wish I knew the truth about what he’s *doing* here. I don’t dislike him, but I dislike not knowing. Does that make any sense or am I just crazy?”

“Yeah. It’s like those religious people that go door to door, the genuinely nice ones. You don’t dislike ’em until they start talking about what’s good for you, what’s going to save your soul, and all that jazz.”

"Yeah, I'm pretty sure he's not a Jehovah's Witness, Marty."

"I *know*, but I'm just saying—"

"" S'okay. I get it. Thanks for trying to understand. Listen, I'm going to fish a bit more, see if I can get one of them to bite. If that doesn't work…I don't know."

"Check his wallet," suggested Marty.

"I don't think he has one."

"What? No money? No credit cards?"

She shrugged, then realized how dumb that was. "It's like I said—he's mysterious."

"Rosie, *everyone* carries *something* around with them. Where's he staying?"

"Good question." Why hadn't she asked Bellamy that? It's like her stellar PI skills became frazzled around him. "I'll find out."

"Follow him if you have to. Be discreet. Remember what Eddie and I showed you about getting someone away from a place you want to search?"

"Uh-huh. I should report *you* to the cops, you pair of derelicts."

He laughed. "Be careful, though. No need to…okay,

she's here. Gotta go."

"Oh, okay. Unless you want me to explain that complimentary blow-job—"

He hung up before she could finish. Rose smirked to herself, slid her Smartphone back into her jeans pocket, and considered her next move, one she'd decided upon as soon as Marty had mentioned breaking and entering. Hers would be an even scummier trick, so scummy, in fact, that she was surprised Marty himself hadn't suggested it. The very thought of bugging her mom's room to listen in on private conversations set her stomach on fire. Curiosity, though, was to ethics what a hard-on was to a jock-strap: the bigger one grew, the more the other had to stretch. And right now, where Bellamy was concerned, she had a serious boner for the truth.

Not just for the truth.

The idea amused her as she made her way back to the front entrance of her mother's house. Bright, orange pre-twilight sunbathed her as she crossed in front of the square lawn between apartment buildings. Rose stopped, raised her face to soak in maybe the last of the day's generous, rejuvenating rays. It was late in the day. Soon they would order supper, hopefully, a Pizza and potato skins, probably not the best thing for her mom's heart condition but it had been a family tradition for years, whenever Rose or Andy came to stay the night.

She noticed a thin shadow roll across the sidewalk up ahead. Its source was probably on the grass in the gap, the next gap, between buildings. At any other time, she wouldn't have given it another thought, but someone *had* been tailing them through the park and likely here as well. No way was she going to pass up this chance.

Rose drew her switchblade and crept toward the gap, hogging the metal fence that guarded the steps to the building's cellar. She heard shoes scuff a hard surface, hushed words, the jangling of keys. Was the asshole stalker chatting with someone on his cell, giving some kind of progress report to whoever had sent him? The idea pissed her off. She squeezed the grip of her knife at her side, with no intention of using it but every intention of making the bastard *think* she would. She stayed to the right of the sidewalk, watching the shadow fidget ahead. Ready to hug the wall as soon as she got past—

The tip of her blade caught the metal fence. *Clink!*

She iced up but then melted to nothing. Said *screw it* to herself and darted out onto the grass in front of the loiterer, all in the space of a single ragged breath.

Pastel green polo shirt, beige trousers, white shoes. It was definitely the same guy who'd followed them through the park—the creepy cyclist her mom had spotted several times at various venues throughout the day. But this time he wasn't wearing shades, and she now had her first really good look at him.

"*You!*"

"Aw, damn it. Rosie, you need to—"

"Alex, what the hell are *you* doing here?" She lowered her blade and, hand on heart, indulged a massive purifying sigh of relief. "Man, you really creeped me out. Don't *do* that."

He had his back to the wall and he looked a little pale. His pockets were hanging out of his trousers. "I'm really sorry, Rosie."

"So you should be! What's the big idea, anyway, stalking me all goddamn day? Did Eddie put you up to this?"

He hemmed, nodding to the opposite wall, somewhere behind her to her right. She turned and heard the click of a gun simultaneously. "Oh, shit."

"That's right, lady." The gunman, a goateed wannabe gangster type in his early thirties, wore a white sleeveless tee and suspenders. He pointed a shiny silver gun at her, horizontally, and stepped out of the shade. "You know this pig?"

She swallowed a mouthful of dry nothing. "Uh, yeah. I do."

"You're an undercover pig, too?"

"No. You've got it wrong, pal. We're PIs." She saw that he had Alex's wallet in his other hand.

He took a few smoothly menacing steps toward her, head tilted slightly as if it was unconsciously trying to mimic the angle he held his weapon. "Five-Oh, PI…P-I-G! Y'all stink the same to me, bee-atch." He motioned her to join Alex against the wall, the spread-eagled wallet still in his hand. "Get your pale bony ass over there. And drop the blade."

She reluctantly obeyed.

"Now," he said, "Tell me what the hell you know."

"Know? About what?" The irony of her

predicament pricked Rose's well-honed sense of the macabre. She shook her head minutely, swore under her breath. Bad enough that this idiot assumed she was working with the same guy who'd been stalking her all day, the same guy who she *did* actually work with at Dobkin & Searle; but now he was convinced *she* was the one doing the stalking, on some kind of cockamamie police sting or stakeout or whatever the hell he'd cooked up in his diseased so-called brain.

"Don't give me any of your crap, lady. Two dicks with badges come sniffing 'round my shit and you say coincidence. I say there's a bullet for each of y'all right here if you don't tell me what you know!"

"Okay, listen—we can prove we're not here for you," said Alex, surprisingly cool considering the Miami Vice style tan on his face was now almost as pale as Rose's natural pasty pallor. "We can prove we don't know you. You've got it all wrong, friend."

She knew Alex was just bullshitting—how could they possibly *prove* they didn't know this guy—but he sounded sincere and plausible and like he was on this asshole's side. It was all about defusing the situation now, with talk, experience, and not wanting to eat a bullet. Rose resolved to let Alex do the talking. He had much more experience as a PI and a lesser propensity for rubbing people up the wrong way. Especially strangers. Yep, she needed to keep her mouth shut.

Unfortunately, the gunman disagreed. "Your turn." He pointed the piece at her forehead from about six feet away. Not close enough for her to try a disarming move. She chewed her bottom lip, struggling to find a clever rejoinder.

The only thing that came to mind was the truth. "You live in the same building as my mom. She's the only reason I'm here."

He blinked at her. "What's her name?"

"Blythe. Blythe Foley, Apartment Four-Twelve. She's lived here for years."

"You're lying. You're with this piece of crap. He was skulking around right outside my…he was all over my stuff."

"He was tailing *me*," she said impatiently. "He's not here for you. He's here for me. Do you get it?"

The gunman spat his incredulity at her, a mixture of anger and black amusement really animating him now.

Rose wanted to explain the whole story to him, but she didn't *know* the whole story. Only Alex did.

"Tell him," she snapped at her colleague. "Tell him why you're here before he does something really dumb."

He might have been a little over six feet, but looking into the muzzle of a revolver, Alex Hydell had never seemed so diminished. Sweat poured from his temples.

"I-it's like she said. I was hired to follow the guy she's with…who her mother's with. I was hiding from them, not from you. I—we don't know you."

"You pricks usually know how to lie your way out of trouble. Guess what? You don't." He took careful aim at Alex, whose defiant grimace and giant panic breaths signaled he knew he was about to die.

"Wait!" Rose threw her hands in the air as the man thrust the piece in her direction again. "What if you're wrong? Do you really want to be *that* guy?"

"Lady, I *am* that guy."

She stole in a breath through frozen lips. For the first time in a long time, she felt the chill of evil around her. This guy had no doubt he was right, had no doubt he had the right to kill them; nothing they said or did would convince him otherwise.

Alex boldly snatched at the gun. But the gunman was ready for him. He hammered the piece down on the back of Alex's neck, dropping him instantly. Then he kicked him several times on the ground. By this point Alex was unconscious, maybe even dead—she couldn't tell.

Rose considered jumping the bastard while he was seeing red, but she left it too long. He stopped kicking Alex and, standing astride him, resumed his original firing posture, the weapon aimed squarely at Rose. The flash of hate in his bugged-out eyes made her shut hers tight and turn her head away.

Oh, God. This is my time. I'm not ready.

"*Eso sería un error*, Miguel."

"What—"

"I think you know what I mean." The speaker sounded far away and incredibly intimate at the same time, as though he were all around them.

Rose looked up. There, on the edge of the grass, as still as a wax figure, Bellamy stood watching the gunman. The urge to scream at him—for Heaven's sake, *he* didn't need to die here as well, the idiot—didn't make it out. She was too appalled by his stupidity, that he was throwing his life away for *no reason.*

The gunman whispered in shock, "It's you?"

To Rose's horror, Bellamy began to walk slowly, almost funereally, across the grass toward them. "Yes, it's me," he replied.

The gunman back-stepped, eyes bugging. "S-stay away from me."

"Stay away from *her.*" Bellamy's eyes turned to darts as he willed the demand on the gunman.

"I-I wasn't going to… I swear."

"Then don't."

"But why are you…?"

"If anything happens to this woman, you'll know the answer to that question."

"Please… I'll disappear. I'll go anywhere. Just stay away from me."

"Then what are you waiting for?"

Terrified, the gunman looked at Rose, then at Bellamy, then down at the weapon by his side. He dropped it on the grass and bolted out of sight.

Coolly, after he gracefully shed the stark demeanor, Bellamy picked it up and handed it to Rose.

"I think you should carry this from now on," he said.

Adrenaline pumped through her body like icy fire and she couldn't seem to find the right words, any words. Instead, she just took it from him.

After checking to make sure Alex was still alive—he was—Bellamy suggested they call for an ambulance. The calmness in his voice and his body language and, hell, everything about him, was unlike anything she'd ever seen. There was no hint of stress. Nothing.

"What the hell just happened?" she demanded. "Who *are* you?"

"Bellamy."

"Bellamy?" she squeaked.

"Rose?"

"Huh?" Her brain was all fuzz and confusion.

"I think you should call for that ambulance."

Her breath was solid in her chest, refusing to let go. "Oh, I'm okay, thanks."

"Not for you. For this man."

"Right, right. Good call." She still stood there,

unmoving. Then suddenly snapped out of a daze. "I mean sure, I'll make the call. Bellamy?"

"Yes, Rose?"

Rose narrowed her eyes at the man. "I think you and I need to have a long talk."

CHAPTER SIX

While the police and the EMS were en route, Rose made Alex comfortable on the grass, with the help of a young man, a neighbor, who'd heard the shouting, glimpsed the gunman, and had immediately dialed 911. The man fetched his kid's *Disney* pillow for Alex to rest his head on. His little daughter peered shyly around the corner. Rose thanked her for the loan of her pillow.

A million questions spun around in her mind as she ran Bellamy's exchange with the gunman, Miguel, over and over in her head. The most obvious: how did they know each other? Why was Miguel so terrified of Bellamy? What bearing did that have on Bellamy's relationship with her mother? Who the hell *was* he?

But she only had time to ask him one question before the ambulance arrived. Her own choice surprised her. "Is there anything you want me to say in my statement, about what happened, I mean?"

If he *was* some sort of gang boss or had influence with criminal types, the cops might not want to hear that the gunman knew him. After all, Bellamy had just saved her life.

"You should tell the truth," he replied, twitching a smile. "But thank you for considering that."

"I owe you one. You're sure you won't get in any trouble?"

"I'll think of something."

And think of something he must have, because the police let him go almost immediately, without even taking his statement. The female officer who spoke to him appeared distracted, a little edgy after he left. What had he said to her? Was he some kind of Confidential Informant, colluding with the cops while working his way up the criminal underworld? Jesus, everyone else in town *but* Rose seemed to know him.

After giving the gun and her statement as evidence,

she went to the hospital to make sure Alex was going to be okay. Sure, the guy had been stalking her family all day, but someone had put him up to it. Someone had hired him. And that same someone must be concerned about what Bellamy was up to.

Alex came around after an hour or so. The doctors finished their tests, told him he'd need to stay for observation for a few days. Several broken ribs, a dislocated shoulder, a cracked collarbone, and concussion. It could so easily have been her lying there, stiff and drifting along on a cocktail of painkillers.

"I told Helen," said Rose. "She'll get in touch with Susan for you. Shouldn't be long."

"Huh?" Alex's expression somewhere far away on a cloud of medication.

Rose rolled her eyes. "I said your wife, Susan, is on the way. She won't be long."

"Aw, yeah. That is so…I can't think of the word. Susie-Q. Kiss you, miss you, Susie-Q," he replied through a series of drugged induced giggles.

Rose cleared her throat, then clicked her fingers to get his attention. "Alex, stay with me. It's Rosie."

"Hey, Rosie. You ride good, you know. Why don't you buy some job…jump…jodhpurs. Yeah, that's 'cause you got nice legs, you know. Women who ride are hot. Real hot. Susie-Q used to ride. I think she—"

"Okay, Alex, I need you to focus. It's important." His glazed eyes flickered open. He didn't seem to know where he was. "You were following me today. That's when you saw me ride. Do you remember?"

"Following you, yeah. You don't look much like your mom, you know. I think you should be careful."

"What? Why do you say that?"

"That guy you were with…"

"Bellamy?"

"Huh?"

"Bellamy. The guy who was with us, the guy you've been following—what do you know about him?"

"A ghost."

The heavy thwump in her stomach nearly knocked Rose off her feet and she swallowed hard against the starchy walls of her throat. "W-what do you mean?"

"I couldn't find any trace of him. My friend in the agency ran his picture through their facial recognition whatchcallit, and…nada."

The odd sensation of relief poured down her back. "That just means he isn't on their system. It doesn't mean he can't be traced."

He sighed, smiling to himself, eyes closed. "Jodhpurs."

"Alex, who hired you to follow him?"

"Ah…Foley."

"Yes, that's my name: Rose Foley. But who hired you to follow us?"

"Axel Foley." He began humming the *Beverly Hills Cop* theme tune. "He's a bit of an a-hole, your brother, if you don't mind me saying. Rosie. Hey, aren't you boning Marty Brigman? The guys in the office all—"

"No. I'm not. What's this about my brother?"

"Your brother…um…he came around the office yesterday, asked me to keep an eye on your mother. He told me not to tell you, said you would—I'm trying to think of the phrase he used—kind of a dickish thing to say if you ask me—something about you being on your menstrual cycle."

"The little shit!" It *did* sound like the sort of thing Andy would say. Wait till she got hold of that pint-sized twad. "Why did he want you to keep an eye on his mom? Was it because of the new guy, the guy we were with in the park today—the ghost?"

"Nope. Axel didn't know who was going to show up."

"You mean Andy."

"*Andy!* That's it. Bit of a dick. He didn't need to go behind your back like that, but he paid upfront, so I took the job. Kinda wish I'd told him to stick his face in the fan."

"Don't worry about that. I'll make sure he does. So, he knew there was someone at my mom's house and he wanted him followed for some reason. Is that right?"

"Correctamundo. My mouth's dry."

"Just one more question, Alex, then I'll get you some water."

"Jodhpurs. Water. Dick. Got it." His eyes rolled in their sockets as he swiveled his head around the room.

"What did my brother think this man was there for?"

"Money. What else? He's some kind of Wills 'n'

Probate Attorney. Least that's what Axel Foley said. He found out his mom had made an appointment to see an attorney, so he hired me to find out who the attorney is. I've been watching the apartment for a few days, but I didn't see him go in through the front door. He's tricky, this attorney. I was right there and he slipped by me somehow. Don't think I'll be going back there." Again, he hummed the *Beverly Hills Cop* theme. Then he fell asleep.

***

It was a lazy, sweaty evening when the light faded. Rose's mom dozed in her favorite armchair, the soporific fan blowing barely cool air across her. Rose couldn't stand to be indoors when it was so humid like this, so, after dunking her face in a sink full of cold water, she grabbed a beach towel and her six-pack of beer from the fridge and trudged up to the rooftop terrace she loved so much. She hoped no one would be up there; alone time was exactly what she needed right now. But her regular spot was occupied.

Damn it.

Some shirtless dude was perched on the edge with his feet dangling over the side. She considered the opposite end of the roof, but the view over there was horrible. Just more apartment buildings and she would be on full display for everyone to see her slowly breaking down. On the verge of giving up, she glimpsed at the shirtless guy again and caught his side profile as he gazed wistfully into the orange and purple sunset.

It was Bellamy.

A gentle fizz of nervous excitement made her smile to herself. Self-consciousness was an old acquaintance, one she'd bested years ago; encountering it now was almost nostalgic. Ditto the girlish flutter in her stomach. But what was it about *this* guy that made her feel so…interested?

The mystery?

The fact that he was such a square *and* a mystery?

Or was it his boyish biker-look cuteness and his cut-from-granite body, without the obnoxious attitude that normally went with them?

Hell, all of the above, she thought as she made her way over. *At the very least, I owe him a beer for saving my life.*

He had a couple of smallish tattoos; one on his shoulder, the other on his right forearm. They suited his look but not his personality from what Rose could tell. It's like the body didn't belong to the person living inside of it.

"Mind if I join you?" she asked, already setting her towel down next to him. "You've actually found my favorite spot."

"Please do." He helped straighten the towel for her. "You come up here a lot?"

"Whenever I get cabin fever in that apartment or when it gets too hot…like tonight."

"You're not afraid of heights, then."

"Nope." She took her Punisher t-shirt off, revealing an old tube top that barely covered her breasts, then removed her clingy jeans so she wore nothing but her boy-cut shorts. The freeing of her clammy skin was refreshing in the humid Nova Scotia summer air. Bellamy watched her slyly from the corner of his eye, as though his libido was at war with his gallantry. It amused her to no end. "What's wrong? Girls are shy where you come from?"

"Not exactly," he replied, ogling her cleavage when she crouched to sit next to him. "They just had a lot more layers to peel off."

"Yeah, I hear the weather's crappy in Britain." She returned the favor, studying his glistening pecs and the line of dark hair leading down from his navel. "There you go." She handed him a beer, then cracked one for herself. It frothed up and spilled down her front. "Shoot!" With quick thinking, Rose immediately began to lap up the spillage. It tasted so good, she downed the full can in one shot. She was about to belch out loud but changed her mind, swallowed it instead, and let the gases ease out the corner of her mouth.

Bellamy was grinning at her. He had a lovely, guileless smile that reminded her of…someone from her past that she couldn't quite place.

"What's wrong?" she asked. "Girls also don't drink where you come from?"

"You're awfully concerned about the girls where I'm from." He took a quick sip. "They drank tea. In china cups."

She rolled her eyes and averted her gaze out to the

landscape in front of them while sparing a peek at him from the corner of her eye. "And the guys?"

He quirked an eyebrow, perceiving her challenge. Then, unexpectedly, he downed his beer in a single, sexy gulp. As soon as he'd finished, Bellamy plucked another can from the plastic rings and lobbed it to Rose.

She laughed and held this one away from her while she cracked the ring cap open. "I should warn you," she told him, "when I drink, I say the first damn thing that comes to mind. Seriously, I'm incapable of holding back. Just so you know."

"By that measure," he replied with a grin, "you've clearly been drinking all day."

Rose gave his arm a gentle punch. "Don't sass *me*, Sunshine. I'm the Queen of Sass. I've got sass tattooed on my…umm…never mind." She wasn't sure how far to take it with him, or how much sarcasm Bellamy would pick up on. "So how did you and my mom first meet?" She hoped the sudden random change of topic might blindside him, get through his defenses, but one beer wasn't enough for that.

"You'll have to ask her," he replied. "We have an agreement."

"Okay, then let's make an agreement. You and me."

"What kind?"

"Truth or dare."

"I don't know what that is," he admitted. "Is it like a game?"

"It is. But it's a binding one. You can't just back out if you're uncomfortable. It's a point of honor."

He gave her a suspicious glance.

"Oh, don't be like that." She tried loosening him up by grabbing his jaw and giving it a gentle wiggle. It seemed to work. He inched closer to her in interest. "Okay, so listen, the rules are simple…" And she explained them, giving examples. Bellamy shook his head in amusement, then took a few swigs from the second can of beer.

"I'm going to regret this," he said, "but all right then. Let's have it."

"Yay."

"Just one condition."

"What's that?"

"I ask you first."

Rose swallowed hard and flushed, all her old insecurities leaking out like vapor through the chinks in her armor. She suddenly felt as if he already knew all of her secrets, that he could see right through her, and that this dumb game was going to end mortifyingly for her.

"Shoot," she said. "Give it your best go."

"Very well." He twitched a smile and set his can down on the concrete ledge between them. "Truth or dare?"

"Truth."

"Do you find me attractive?"

Oh boy.

"You mean on a scale of one to ten?" she asked, her heart beginning to race. "Ten being I want to jump you right here?"

"A simple yes or no will do."

After a short and blank hesitation, she replied, "Yes." Then she backtracked. "Not that I want to jump you right here, right now, or anything, but that's my honest answer."

His stoic response, a simple nod, disappointed her a little, but the more she watched, the more she could sense his relief. It practically emanated from him, not in his body language but through his darkly alluring eyes and, for want of a better word, his very being. Rose not only felt like she shared his secret; she felt as though she *was* his secret. It didn't make sense when she tried to form it into words in her mind. He was here for her mom, not her. And yet this was the question he'd asked her, the first thing he'd wanted to know?

"My turn," she said to break the awkward silence. "Truth or dare?"

He replied without pause, "Dare."

Rose sighed. Of course. No way was he going to choose Truth and tell her what *she* wanted to know, unless…

She sprouted a sly, lopsided grin. "I dare you to tell me the truth about what my mom hired you to do."

He nodded as if he'd been expecting her to try that. "She hired me to be her chauffeur."

"But you don't even drive. And she doesn't have a car."

"So, you see how she saves on gas."

"You know what? You're starting to lighten up. I

think you may have a sarcastic bone somewhere in there after all."

He handed her another beer in reply. "Truth or dare?"

"Dare," she replied, more at ease now.

"Very well. I dare you to have lunch with me tomorrow."

Rose cracked open another can. "You mean go out…just the two of us?"

"Yes."

"I don't want to leave—"

"Your mother won't be on her own. Your brother will be here, will he not?"

"Beats me." She checked her cell for messages. Oddly enough, Andy had sent her a text only a few minutes ago. It said he'd be there before noon tomorrow. She looked up at Bellamy, her vision swimming a little after chugging two-and-a-half beers in a matter of minutes. "How the hell did you know that?"

"Know what?"

"That Andy had…" Rose dismissed the idea as absurd. This guy was no more psychic than he was a chauffeur. But there was definitely something special about him, something she couldn't quite put her finger on. A quiet but strong pull. A center of gravity. A kind of calm inevitability. He just didn't…belong. But she sensed he *wanted* to belong. Somewhere. To someone.

"Okay, we'll do lunch," she told him. "But first you have to tell me something about yourself."

"Like what?"

"I don't know. Anything. Something important that happened to you. One of your secrets. Just give me *something* to work with, gawd. You've been with me all day and I know almost nothing about you."

He set his beer down again, pulled his feet up, and sat cross-legged instead. The way he gazed out toward the sunset filled her imagination with wild fantasies and speculations. Literally nothing about his past, no matter how far-fetched, would have surprised her in that moment. He was all of her most elusive investigative quarries rolled into one. He was a guy she'd never written about in her magazine pieces because she hadn't known guys like him even existed in the postmodern mass media age. He was un-self-conscious. Unrehearsed. He didn't feel the need to sell himself the whole time and it was beyond refreshing.

And he was smoking hot to boot.

"You're right, Rose. I have been keeping too much from you."

"Uh-huh. You think? Both of you have. It's driving me nuts."

"There's only so much I can say without her permission…"

"I don't mean you should reveal anything privileged. That's not what I'm asking. Not yet, anyway." She threw him a wink, which seemed to light him up inside. "Just tell me something pivotal that happened to you."

"In that case," he said, "you should make yourself comfortable."

"Ooh, is it an epic story?" She shuffled a little closer to him.

"Not for the faint of heart."

"You're hyping this up. It better be a blockbuster, Bud. Lunch is at stake."

He turned to face her, the sunset's reflection

kindling unfathomable mystery in the dark pools of his eyes. The deeper Rose gazed, the fiercer the light seemed to burn. It enlarged, rising out of the darkness like twin molten circles on the end of an invisible brand. It mesmerized her, unlike anything she'd ever known. There was something wonderful yet terrifying inside the burning ringlets, a powerful secret no man or woman had a right to know. But she couldn't stop herself from looking deeper into the emptiness as it seemed to gaze back at her. She leaned in, wanting a taste of the darkness, her heart demanding it. Bellamy lifted his hand and cupped her face, his thumb caressing the line of her jaw, and then tickled the edge of her lower lip. Her eyes closed as her face neared his.

Then…Rose was gone. Taken by the sudden depths of the darkness that crashed down over her.

***

A cannonball hurtled toward her face; if it weren't for the inferno behind, silhouetting it for that brief second, the projectile would have knocked her head clean off. But she threw her body down onto the deck and stayed low when a wooden pole splintered a few feet from where she'd been standing, two sharp pieces daggering into her thigh and shoulder. After the quick jabs of pain lessened to a hot throbbing, she only felt angry. Frightened and angry and utterly determined to do her part, whatever the cost.

It was something she'd never felt before, not with this intensity.

There was a constant roar beneath the rapid thunderclaps. Ships-of-the-line and frigates alike battered each other with awesome ferocity. The sun had set but the flames from burning vessels kept the night in a deadly twilight, just bright enough for each ship to see one another and unleash hell. Her ship fired a broadside at the line of fixed French vessels as it passed, completely wrecking at least one from stern to bow. An alien thrill washed over her. Adrenaline muffled the pain from her wounds. The Rear-Admiral's action, flanking the unsuspecting French fleet like this, was not only working, it was a stroke of genius.

She cried "Huzzah!" with the rest of her crew when

the topmast of one of the biggest enemy ships toppled and came crashing down.

Aboukir Bay was about to go down in history as a great British victory.

She didn't know how she knew all this, the knowledge was foreign to her, but the emotions—pride, fear, elation, even hate—were as real to her as any she'd ever experienced. Sailing was something she'd always *wanted* to try but had never quite gotten around to. Why, then, did it suddenly feel as natural to her as riding a bus? Why did she take such delight in the carnage her side was inflicting on the other? It had to be a dream, but it was all too vivid for comfort.

Her mom had clearly told her way too much about these famous naval engagements of the past. She knew the Nile emptied into this bay, just as she knew Bonaparte would throw a hissy fit when he found out his Mediterranean fleet had been smashed by the British.

From the corner of her eye, she glimpsed the sight of her captain, standing resolutely near the mainmast, his one hand cupped to his mouth as he bellowed orders to the sailors. Through the veil of thick cannon smoke, a pair of sharpshooters of a nearby enemy ship took careful aim. They were still, almost hidden by the tendrils of torn sheets hanging over them. But the flashes from another attack reflected off the flintlocks of their rifles and told her they were close, very, very close to her captain. At that range, they would not miss.

Rose yelled to him but couldn't even hear herself over the thunder. Before she knew it, she was halfway there, the splinter wounds hacking at her arm and leg. Nothing else mattered except reaching her captain in time. No one else had seen the threat. It was up to her, and her alone, to act. A thin smoke cloud obscured the assassins, but only for a moment. They were hunkered down in the webbed netting, their sights zeroed on the big prize.

Twin flashes branded the smoke.

The first shot tore through her chest like a hot, savage beast. It knocked the wind from her body and spun her around. The second buried itself in her lower back and she collapsed onto her captain. In his one eye, blazed the passion of brotherhood. With his one arm, he tried to hold her upright, but a spasm of pain flailed up her spine and then vanished. After that…she felt nothing.

He spoke comforting words to her that she couldn't hear. He looked away and issued orders she couldn't comprehend. Orders that Rose wanted to repeat at the top of her lungs, as per her role as an officer in the Navy. The ship lurched with the weight of another violent attack. She staggered out of his grasp and spilled over the side and plunged toward the sea, holding her chest. During the fall she thought of home, a place she should know but didn't. The feeling of home seeped out potently, though. It translated across time, across oceans, and across the mortal barrier, she now knew. It was different for every person, but it existed deep inside of everyone, a universal identity nothing could take away. The battle raged all around her, but it grew distant, an echo of things that mattered in a muted tunnel with no walls—miles and leagues away.

The Battle of the Nile faded to a blurred mural and froze in time, like one of those dramatic paintings her mom had shown her when she was young.

That falling sensation suddenly snapped her back to her own reality and she was once again on the rooftop where she had her rendezvous with Bellamy. To her horror, Rose realized she'd fallen asleep up there. Bellamy had left her? Then, with a start, she accidentally toppled over the edge…

She screamed until her back seemed to smack against the rickety bed of her mother's guest room.

"Rose?"

Hearing her mom's voice came with a sensation of confusion and relief all at the same time. She sat straight up in bed, covered in a thick sheen of sweat and immediately felt for the bullet wounds in her back and chest, then for the splinter wounds in her shoulder and thigh.

Nothing.

"Rose? Is everything okay?"

Her heart jackhammered against her chest bone and reverberated back through her lungs. She glanced around her old room, mentally clutching at the fixtures and the colors and the ambiance…anything familiar that she could use to anchor herself to this reality.

"A bad dream?" Her mom poked her head around the door, leaning in further and looking concerned. Rose couldn't remember the last time she'd been asked that question by anyone. How long since she'd had such a vivid nightmare? Not since childhood. Rose rarely remembered her dreams, but she knew she'd never forget this one. Not in a million years.

"The Battle of the Nile," she said, sipping from the glass of water someone had kindly placed on her bedside table. "I took a bullet for my ship's captain, then I…died."

"Oh." Her mom stared at her. "Then you've just earned yourself an extra pancake, sweetie. Get up and collect thy prize."

She forced as mile toward the old woman. "Be right out." Rose thought back to the rooftop. "Uh, Mom?"

"Yes?"

"How did I…?" On second thought, she didn't want her mom knowing that she'd gotten so shit-faced the night before that she'd had to be carried down all those flights of stairs to her bed. "Never mind. Pancakes sound good."

"And orange juice. Should help take the edge of

that hangover."

"Oh, great," Rose replied sarcastically. "That guy still around?"

"He's in the kitchen, gorging himself on maple syrup. I've never seen anyone swallow a whole bottle of the stuff. You'd better hurry or there'll be none left."

"I'll kill him if there isn't." She tossed the bed sheet off, cringed a little when she saw that she only wore her underwear. How many drinks had she had? Bellamy had to have carried her down in quite a state. Maybe she'd been babbling over her beer, saying things she shouldn't have. Perhaps she'd continued with the game of Truth or Dare long past her responsible limit and had gotten…annoying. Who the hell knew? She couldn't remember a thing after he'd promised to tell her something about himself.

She got dressed in a daze, splashed her face with cold water, then steeled herself for a potentially mortifying encounter with Bellamy. A man whose opinion of her she actually kind of gave a damn about.

"Morning, Rose." He was dressed a little less like a

dork today with a navy blue polo shirt and khaki shorts. And unlike her, he showed no signs of a hangover. In fact, he looked mighty tasty.

"Morning. Sorry about last night." For whatever she'd done. His response might tell the rest.

"No need to be. It was humid up there. And it was the end of a long day."

"Thanks for, you know, not leaving me up there."

"My pleasure. Did you have a peaceful sleep?" The glint in his eye suggested he knew more than he was letting on, but about what?

"I wouldn't say that exactly. But it sure was…educational."

"Oh? In what way?"

"In a way my mom would be proud of. She taught history, you know." Rose eyed him curiously.

"Yes, I know."

"Do *you* know history, Bellamy?" Why couldn't she shake the sense of scrutiny she felt around him?

"Some."

"British history?"

He lobbed another massive forkful of pancake in his mouth and shoved it to the side. "One of my favorite subjects actually."

Rose grabbed ahold of the new maple syrup bottle before he could get to it. "How about the Napoleonic Wars?" she asked.

He beamed at her, then looked down at his plate of scrambled eggs and bacon, trying to hide his enthusiasm. It didn't work. She knew he knew *something* about her dream last night, but what exactly? Was it linked to something he'd told her on the rooftop? And was she nuts for even thinking of the possibility? It seemed crazy.

"How much do you know about the Battle of the Nile?" she asked him.

"I vaguely recall it from when I was young. It's like I told you last night. Hearing those stories of the great British sea commanders inspired me to join the Navy. Admiral Nelson was definitely one of my heroes."

"You were in the Navy?" For the life of her, she couldn't remember him saying that. It made her feel like a complete douchebag. What other personal things had he told her about himself that she'd gone and drowned in a sea of Coors Light. But…there'd only been a six-pack between them. Three each. That had never been enough to slide her into a stupor before. Not even as a teenager. And if he'd been telling her these things, he must have thought she was conscious enough to take them in.

It made no sense.

"For a time," he began. "I was an officer, a lieutenant. But when I was wounded, it forced me…uh…onto a new career path."

"And you told me all this last night, didn't you?"

"At some length," he replied, casting her a half-winking, half-reprimanding look.

"Sorry. I must have been more far-gone than I thought." But she'd only had a few beers. "Maybe I had a bit of heatstroke from the day." Rose flinched when her mother brushed the plate against her arm. On it was a delicious combination of scrambled eggs, bacon, and pancakes. Blythe narrowed her eyes at Rose, as if to say, *what have I told you about drinking too much?*

"We'll have to carry on that conversation sometime," she added to Bellamy, even though deep down she could tell something was missing from last night—something besides her beer-fueled black hole—a missing piece in *his* version of events. No way had she been that drunk when he'd begun to tell her his pivotal thing. She'd been gazing into his gorgeous eyes when she'd seen the two fiery circles and then, just like that, she'd been in the midst of a battle?

It was feasible, even probable, that her unconscious had fashioned that intense dream from what he'd told her just before she'd passed out, and that her brain had linked it to one of her mom's nautical stories of Nelson at war. But why had it seemed so real? Crazy real. As real as anything she'd ever experienced.

Who the heck *was* this guy? The more answers he gave, the more she questioned *herself*, her own sanity, her own feelings, what she wanted him to be. The closer she got to him, the more mysterious he became.

She needed to clear her head, damn it, otherwise, she'd go nuts before the day was out.

Her mom kept slipping into the living room to peer down through the window. After about the eighth or ninth time, she returned wearing a big sunny grin and blurted out, "Okay, you two, he's here!" Gripping the back of Bellamy's chair, she dropped her smile and suddenly looked flustered, chewing her bottom lip. "I know it's going to be awkward—we all know what he's done—but it's important to me that you let me deal with it in my own way. I'm looking at you, Rose. I know you two don't exactly see eye to eye—"

"Or anything to anything. The little shit."

"But bear in mind this might be the last time we are all together as a family. Whatever Andy did, he did it because he was worried about me."

"No, he didn't," Rose shot back. "He hired a PI because he's a selfish little turd who's—"

"Don't. Please don't. Not now, okay? You know I don't ask for much—I never have—but I'm asking you this one time, please don't say anything about it. Don't provoke an argument. I need today to go smoothly, just this once. Let me take the best possible memory of you both with me. That's all I ask."

"But Mom, you're talking like this is it—like you've given up." Rose immediately regretted saying that. It sounded so childish. Between the two of them, only one was in denial about what was going to happen. *Going to happen soon, whether I like it or not.* "Sorry," she added. "You're right. Of course, I won't start anything. He's all yours."

"Thank you. It means a lot."

"' S'okay." Rose turned to Bellamy. "I don't suppose we need to tell you to bite your tongue, Hornblower?"

He didn't reply, probably because he was munching on a mouthful of syrup-soaked pancakes. The sugary sap glistened around his lips and Rose all but reached out to wipe it off.

Or lick it off.

She shivered the thought away just as there was a knock on the door. Several irritating knocks in that rapid-fire signature sequence Andy had somehow never grown out of. As her mom let the moron in, Rose got up and quickly hid the packs of hot chocolate powder he always made a beeline for; he never drank tea or coffee, only hot chocolate, and she wasn't about to pass up her time-honored petty torments for her baby brother.

Bellamy threw her a quizzical look as if to say, *you promised not to start any shit.*

Rose flicked her eyebrows up at him. "Watch and learn, *muchacho*. Watch and learn."

CHAPTER SEVEN

Andy breezed in like he'd just returned from hanging out at the shop corner with his pals, that cocky macho vibe he gave off, especially for the girls, still emanating from him. But when he saw Bellamy he stopped dead and looked the new guy up and down a few times with his baby blue eyes, his thick black eyebrows narrowing.

"And *you* are?"

"Eating breakfast," Rose answered for him.

Her brother glared at her. "I'm not talking to you."

She rolled her eyes and stabbed her fork through a stack of pancakes. "How unfortunate."

"Keep out of this, Rosie. I'm serious. I'm asking

this guy a question."

Bellamy stood and wiped his hand against his shirt before extending it out toward Andy. "Good day. My name is Bellamy. I'm here to help your mother assort her affairs. Won't you join us for some breakfast?" He then looked to Rose's mother to make sure that was alright.

"Of course," she replied. "There's plenty to go around."

Andy didn't budge. He hovered in the doorway, glaring across at their new guest like he was a Russian spy who'd infiltrated the family home while Andy had been away. "Why are you still here?"

"It's like he said," answered Blythe, "he's helping me out for a while."

"With what?" Andy whined.

"Things."

"Uh-huh." Andy thrust a threatening finger at Bellamy. "I'm onto you. I know what you're up to."

"Oh really?" The unguarded taunt in Rose's expression never failed to wind him up, she knew, especially when he was in a mood like this. "Do enlighten us, little brother."

Andy paused for a moment. "I-I hear things, that's all."

"Like what?" asked Rose, challengingly.

"Like he's been sniffing around Mom's finances, and that he won't leave her alone until he gets what he wants. I can't be the only one who calls bullshit on the timing of all this. Tell me you don't smell a rat, Rosie. Seriously, you're sitting here having breakfast with some random guy who's trying to screw us over…screw *Mom* over, I mean." She could see the slightest hint of blush color his cheeks as he attempted to recover the statement.

Bellamy didn't stop chewing, nor did he look up at his accuser. A part of Rose wanted him to defend himself, but she knew he probably wouldn't. And against her better judgment—Andy's concerns were not unfounded—she found herself taking Bellamy's side. For one thing, he'd saved her life when he'd scared off that gunman.

For another, it seemed to mean a great deal to her mom that Bellamy stayed by her side. And thirdly, Rose's interest in him had become far more than mere curiosity. He was someone she felt she could weirdly trust, wanted to trust, with her mom's life *and* her own, and that was worth defending against her selfish little skeez of a brother.

"He's not a bad guy," she told Andy with a reluctant sigh, "once you get to know him."

"*What?* You actually *approve* of what he's doing?"

"Tell me what he's doing wrong," answered Rose, looking to her mom for permission to continue this line of defense. The nod and the proud smile she received buoyed her up more than any editorial praise she'd gotten as a columnist. "I mean really, what's your problem? Mom has invited him to spend time with her, to help her sort some things out. Why should that get your panties in a twist, hotshot?"

Andy stormed over to the cupboard and rummaged around for his hot chocolate. "Mom, please don't tell me you're all out of—"

"This what you're looking for, dingus?" Rose tossed him the packs, not wanting to stir things up any more than they already were. She'd underestimated her brother's directness, his sheer lack of tact with such a delicate situation. Did he *have* no shame? Hiring a PI from *her own firm* to spy on them before he got here?

Words failed.

"When are you gonna grow up?" he snapped at her and then glanced between her and Bellamy with a wave of realization. "Oh, wait a minute. This is precious." He held his hands up and the knowing grin spread across his face. "I can see it all over you," motioning to Rose and then Bellamy. "You two are a thing, right?"

"What are you yammering about?" Rose snapped back in defense.

"That's the only way this all makes sense. He comes here spinning his lawyer's web, twists Mom round his little finger till he gets her finances right where he wants them, then you show up. And I bet you asked the exact same questions I'm asking. But you're not so vulnerable as Mom, not quite so gullible. You wouldn't fall for all that legal jammer. So, he knew he had to get around you some other way. All he had to do was speak to someone at your firm and they'd tell him what he needed to know."

"Oh yeah? And what's that?"

"Well, let's just say you're not the shining beacon of virtue Mom thinks you are."

She narrowed her eyes. "Explain."

"Marty Brigman. Apparently, his wife sticks little pins in a doll-sized version of you, on account of you and Marty getting all Fifty Shades of Nasty."

Rose shot to her feet, spilling the chair off its feet behind her. "You sick little shit. Who told you that crap? Do you believe everything you hear?"

By this time, her mom was propped against the countertop, arms folded, staring at the floor and shaking her head. This wasn't how the reunion was supposed to have gone *at all*. But how much of that was Rose's fault? Not a whole lot, she reckoned. The little snot had burst in and self-righteously laid down the law like the goddamn Spanish Inquisition, without acknowledging his own family treachery.

"Never mind who told me. So, is it true, about you and…this slippery sonofabitch?"

Still no reaction from Bellamy. Either he was in a Zen-like state of maple syrup-fueled nirvana or he was happy to let a woman fight his battles for him. Rose hurled a coaster at her brother and was about to let fly with both fists when the mystery man, the center of all this family angst, set his knife and fork down on the plate with a clink. It was a sound that wouldn't have disturbed a fly from his plate, but for some reason, Rose and Andy both spun to face him and stayed silent while he calmly spoke.

"I think you owe your mother an apology, Andrew."

Rose's little brother started forward at him but stopped suddenly and began to settle back against the sink just inches from the guest. He swallowed. Couldn't take his eyes off Bellamy. "I-I don't know what you mean."

"You hired a private investigator to follow me, to find out how I was swindling your mother."

"No, I…" He dipped into his jeans pocket for his cell phone. As soon as he pulled it out, Bellamy reached over with one long, muscular arm and slipped it from his grasp—a crime equivalent to severing a limb in Andy's world. But again, Rose's kid brother didn't overreact, didn't throw a mental hissy fit. He simply let this stranger disarm him, all the while maintaining eye contact.

"Go on," said Bellamy, daring Andy to dance around the lie.

"As I was saying…" The first quivers of remorse

trembled Andy's boyish, sun-kissed face. "I was just worried you were being taken for a ride, Mom. I-I was only looking out for you."

"It's all right, sweetie," replied Blythe warmly.

No, it's not, Rose wanted to add, but the soothing air that had descended on the kitchen felt like a salve on her desire to get even. Hers was not the right way to approach this, she knew that. She and Andy, if left to it, would only burn the situation to a crisp. What it needed was a touch of maple syrup.

"Why not ask your mother directly?" Bellamy asked him. "Why betray her trust like that? She's never been anything but honest with you."

Blythe cast Bellamy a sharp glance, as if to rebuke him, but instead said, "We can leave it there. Andy and I can talk about it later. There's no more that needs to be said now."

"Very well," Bellamy replied with a curt nod, "If you'll excuse me," then he got up and left the room. On his way out, he turned and subtly motioned for Rose to follow him with the tip of his head. A butterfly sensation in her stomach told her it was something she absolutely wanted to do—go and be alone with this extraordinary and mysterious man—but she wasn't quite finished in the kitchen.

She strode over to her brother, scooping up the plastic bottle of maple syrup on the way, and squirted a little into his face. Then she kicked his ankle and caused Andy to fall flat on his ass.

"That's for calling me a slut, and for going behind my back," Rose shot down at him. "Next time, man up and come to us first."

Blythe threw her hands up and shook her head in despair, then bent down to help Andy. "Why do I bother?" she said aloud.

Rose's pang of regret for helping ruin her mom's big family reunion made her sick to her stomach, but only for a moment. When she saw Bellamy waiting for her in the next room she felt better. Surer that things would turn out okay. That was a very strange feeling to have at a time like this, with her mom being so close to the end, but Rose couldn't help it.

"Are you ready for our lunch date?" he asked her.

She approached his side and couldn't help but smile. The way he stood up to Andy and defended her mom's honor…it was hot. All she wanted at the moment was for Bellamy to take her in his arms and ravage her.

"We just finished breakfast," she replied, trying to hide the eagerness in her voice.

Bellamy placed a hand on Rose's hip and the warmth of his touch made a burning handprint on her skin. His very touch sent her body to the top, all her senses on high alert. In a good way. In a way she never really experienced before.

"Well, I was hoping to spend the day with you. If you'll have me, of course."

Rose swallowed hard, a dry choke of air that elicited no verbal response. All she could do was nod and let Bellamy's hand remain where it was as she made her way to her room. There was just something about this guy…

Something she couldn't get enough of.

Besides, her mind was tumultuous and the emotional weather in her mom's apartment would only make it worse if she stayed. Bellamy, on the other hand, felt like the eye of the storm. He was almost supernaturally cool. Had been all along, whether dealing with the gunmen, the cops, with her own prickly behavior when she'd first met him or with Andy just now. The latter was perhaps her favorite of all because he'd defended her mom like someone out of a history book would have done, appealing to decency and chivalry and respect for one's elders and other out-of-fashion things a brat like Andy would dismiss with an eye-roll and a bored "whatever."

She put her black and white Converses on and grabbed her wallet from the drawer in her bedside table. Then she called into the kitchen on her way out, told her mom she'd be back sometime later that day.

No reply.

Rose led Bellamy down the several flights of stairs to the ground floor, occasionally glancing back and catching his eye. They didn't speak. His golden hair was a little less tidy than it had been yesterday. His movements seemed slightly looser, too, freer and faster, more spontaneous, as though he was trying to copy her. It was an unusual energy. Almost enthusiastic. It made her like him even more because she could tell he enjoyed being with her.

Rose smiled at him. His returning grin spread to his

eyes, and he couldn't help it. A youthful beam shone through the experience. He looked more like a surfer than ever, or some kind of athlete. One of those guys who'd started early and been really good at his chosen profession for so long that he had the wisdom of someone twice his age and an infectious enthusiasm that would always be there.

"Where shall we go?" he asked when they hit the sidewalk. It was another hot and sunny day. Rose wished she'd brought her shades, but she didn't want to go back up to the apartment and grab them.

She shrugged. "Where would you like to go? I'm easy." She immediately winced at the poor choice of words. But he never picked up on it. Or, if he did, never took the opportunity to say anything.

Bellamy thought for a few moments. "Is there a river nearby? Or a boating lake?"

"Aha. Navy guy, right?" She squeezed his shoulder. It was tense, muscular. It felt good in her grasp. "Hornblower missing his water. I get it. If you want, I could pick us up some fast food or something on the way. I think I know just the place."

To her surprise and secret delight, he offered her his

arm.

She hesitated, staring at him. "Why are you such a gentleman?"

"Why do you think?" He backed his words up with confidence in his eyes that practically overwhelmed her. He'd summoned it from somewhere, and it was potent.

Still, she hesitated. Weren't things crazy enough already without her falling for the guy who'd crazied them up in the first place? "But why?" she reiterated. It was an unanswerable question. One she always hated to get asked herself.

"Why not?" He smiled warmly, but a bit devilishly. There was a gravity behind it, a sincerity. Bellamy was not cunning or treacherous. He was just honest. And honestly on its own could be quite charming.

She took his arm, happy to have their bodies touching in any way, and sidled up against him so that their hips and shoulders touched. Again, it felt so good. Too good. Electric even. Risky and safe at the same time. She noticed then that they were a similar height. He was maybe an inch taller, and quite a bit heavier with muscle mass. She'd seen how cut Bellamy was last night on the rooftop. He had to work out at a gym or something. Either that or he spent most of his free time playing sports. No way could a lawyer or a bean-counter stay in such good shape otherwise.

She led him up the street. "You ever been married, Bellamy?"

"Yes. A long time ago, back in England. She was...her name was Alice."

"Divorced."

He sighed. "Hmm."

"But an amicable one, right? You parted as friends?"

He looked at her with simple wonder. "How did you know that?"

"Not sure. Intuition." She quirked a grin his way. "You're frustratingly hard to dislike, you know."

He laughed. "I think that's the nicest thing you've said to me yet."

"Ouch." Rose gave his arm a playful shake and then sighed heavily. "Yeah, I can be a bitch, I know."

"Not from where I stand."

Rose rolled her eyes at him. "You're sweet. But most people would disagree with you."

"Most people have decided who you are at first

glance. You make an impression, Rose."

"Gee, thanks. Is one glimpse all it takes? Why don't you say what you really think?" She was being facetious, but there was also truth somewhere in there. People really *did* peg her as some kind of moody, emo slut in record time, had for years.

So why hadn't Bellamy?

She'd been aggressively hostile to him from minute one, but he'd never displayed anything but affection toward her. "I didn't mean that," she added. "You're not like most other guys."

"I'm not?"

"No. I have no idea how to describe you. That's how much you're not like them."

"That's a good thing, then?" It appeared to be a genuine question.

"Uh-huh. Of course."

He stopped her. The street was quiet. A pungent scent from the gaping flowers on a tree in the middle of the road infused her nose. The sun's heat kissed her pale shoulders and the back of her neck.

"Rose, I have a question to ask you. It's important. It could...change things."

She began to slowly pull away, but he held firm. Weighty questions were almost never welcome ones in her experience, and this guy was her mother's confidante at a crucial time in their lives.

"Important how? In what way?"

He looked away at a stray dog venturing across the road then seemed to stare off at nothing. His confidence seemed to have momentarily deserted him. He clearly didn't like the question any more than she would.

"It might sound strange," he said, "but I'd like to know—no, I *need* to know—how you feel. About me."

She mentally scrambled to find his angle, what she thought he wanted her to say. "Is this a 'would you date me if I asked you' question, or something else?"

"You decide."

"Okay." She thought back over the last twenty-four hours, choosing moments and impressions and feelings like a fruit-picker whose criteria for selecting has already decided how the final dish will taste. "I feel like you want to tell me a secret," she told him. "But either you can't or my mom won't let you.

Whatever it is, I don't think it's a deal-breaker. I think it's between you and her, and if it's important enough that I know, she'll tell me. Like I said, I feel awkward describing you 'cause you're not like anyone I've ever met." She stopped to take a deep breath and smooth out her thoughts. "What I'm saying is, I think I'd date you if you asked me. So…ask me."

Bellamy turned to face Rose directly and leaned in towards her face, slowly. For a moment, she thought he would kiss her. He opened his mouth to respond but nothing came out.

"Hold that thought," she said, inching her face even closer to him, her lips aimed at his. He watched her with those dark, intriguing eyes that appeared to shimmer with invitation. He leaned in and met her the rest of the way.

Then they kissed.

It was neither anxious nor cautious but somewhere in between. Curiosity. Expectation. Adventure. Excitement. Like a jump off a dizzying ledge into a sparkling blue sea. They came up for air, then went under again.

And again.

Rose couldn't remember his question. Only the answer, and it was the right one.

CHAPTER EIGHT

The harbor front was a longish bus ride away because Rose's mom lived outside the city. A short distance by map, but the route incorporated several bizarre detours that made the journey a bit of trek. Luckily, Bellamy was quite the conversationalist. After their passionate embrace in the streets, he seemed to open up and brighten like a newly formed flower. His attitude was infectious.

He told her fascinating stories about some of the people he'd met in his line of work. They always seemed to be elderly people, mostly, which fit her assumption that he was some kind of high-end financial adviser for wills and estates. But he'd clearly gotten to know his clients very well, even intimately, which struck her as unusual for someone in that profession. He was also way too young to have seen so much, met so many people, and to have been married "a long time ago".

Rose warmed to his enthusiasm, though. The closer they got to the water, the more animated he became, swiveling this way and that to snatch glimpses of the harbor through the gaps between buildings and trees, or telling her repeatedly how much he'd missed the sounds of sailing.

This was his element. It was obvious before they got to the farmer's market by the pier, and it was written all over him as he cast their rowboat's rope off the wooden dock (refusing the rental guy's offer to help) and hopped aboard, instantly finding his sea legs as he settled the little boat's violent rocking caused by Rose's oh so graceful slide off her seat and onto her butt, damn near tearing an oar out of its fixture. Even after her relentless cursing, which would out-salt any sailor's, didn't dampen the moment for him. Bellamy gently lifted Rose to her feet and made her comfortable. Then he grinned like a little kid as he took the oars and steered the boat out with strokes as natural as any she'd ever seen. His muscles pulling tightly underneath his blue polo shirt. She couldn't help but stare.

"You row us out, I'll row us back," she offered, admiring his skill but at the same time eager to show him that she had a little of her own, that she could handle herself on the water. If this was so important to him, she strangely wanted to be a part of it.

"Where shall we head?" he asked.

"The boat guy mentioned a few small islands just over there, around the bend." She pointed the way. "He said people sometimes get out and look around. I hope it isn't too busy. Nothing worse than being on a secluded island than having other freaking people there."

"Robinson Crusoe might disagree with you."

"That's because he was alone. But if a hot young lady had been shipwrecked with him, you can bet..."

"He'd have told his rescuers to keep on swimming. That way." Bellamy pointed down to the depths where the harbor's mouth opened to the ocean.

Rose laughed. "Now you're getting it." She gave him

a coy grin and he couldn't help but return it. The curve of his mouth was hypnotizing to her. "There's no better fantasy, am I right?"

"You're not wrong." The way he checked her out this time, her neck and trailing down, with a devilish curl of his lips, was such a turn-on that she could almost see the erotic scene playing out in his mind. She could tell he fought with the thoughts, that they conflicted with his deeply embedded morals and gentlemanly ways.

Now she wished she'd brought some kind of swimsuit. The skimpier the better. It wasn't her usual *modus operandii* for scoring with a guy—her skin had always been pale as winter, whereas most men preferred the bronzed look—but this was an opportunity she didn't want to miss. He definitely wanted her. That much had been obvious for some time now. But he was reluctant to make his move, for whatever reason. So, Rose decided that it was up to her to seal this deal. One way or another, they were going home from this outing fully acquainted. As many times as he could handle her.

The island they selected was the least accessible of

the three. One tiny sand cove, barely big enough for their boat to fit into, was the only place for them to land. After Bellamy had dragged the little boat onto the beach, Rose swerved the stern around so that the boat rested diagonally across the cove, blocking anyone else from landing there.

"Sneaky," he told her, his eyes burning with…something.

"But necessary." Rose ignored the butterflies in her stomach and threw him a wink as she plucked the picnic hamper out. Bellamy strolled ahead up the rocky verge into the stubby trees, showing no signs of the exerting row across the water he'd just made. Rose found herself staring once again, unable to rip her eyes from his tall figure. She found his ripped, athletic surfer type body fascinating because it didn't seem to belong to the overly polite, stilted manner he projected. Maybe it was all an act. Whatever the case, it was definitely one of the things that attracted her to him. Bellamy didn't seem to fit into any mold she knew. It was like she had discovered a whole new species of man.

But he did seem to fit in here, on this remote island,

on the water. That much she could tell from the way he relaxed and absorbed the air around them.

"Shall I pick a spot for us?" he called back with that boyish enthusiasm, breaking her from the dreamlike trance.

"Go for it. Somewhere out of view."

"Whatever the lady desires," Bellamy replied with a mocking bow.

She rolled her eyes because his weird phrases weren't a pretention, like in some TV drama. No, etiquette and protocol were important to him for some reason, they must have had a real place somewhere in his upbringing. But the best part was he didn't take himself too seriously.

"Much obliged, kind sir," she replied in an attempt to copy his manner.

Bellamy glanced over his shoulder at her and smiled yet again, something he didn't seem to be able to help doing. Rose melted a little and forced herself to look away, to hide her meager vulnerable side.

The spot he picked was a small grassy area under the trees, ringed by a shallow verge on three sides. A layer of rock moss made it soft underfoot. On the open side, a thicket of rhododendron bushes shielded them from the lake. The sound of water lapping against the rocks not far below was soothing. Hypnotic. A flock of mallards flying low over the trees made no noise whatsoever.

Bellamy crouched beside her as she laid the tablecloth on the ground and emptied the picnic contents onto it. When she'd finished, he took her by the hand; lacing their fingers sent delicate waves of delight through her fingertips.

"You did good," she murmured, dumbly trying to keep the banter going. Nervous, all of a sudden. "Nice spot, I mean."

"I thought you'd like it."

After a few tense moments, he let go and sat cross-legged opposite her on the blanket. Watching her with a lingering curiosity.

Stay cool. No pressure, she thought. He was playing this like a gentleman, but the problem was she'd never been able to play it like a lady. Usually, by the time it got to this stage in a date, she'd be all over the guy. But a part of her knew better than to make him rush it. Christ, she just wanted to wrap her arms around him and kiss every smoking inch of his body while making love to him over and over.

Damn, this etiquette thing was going to kill her.

Rose tore the packaging off the BLT sandwiches and handed him one. "I hope you're hungry."

"Famished. But what's in this?"

She smiled, remembering he was a fish out of water. "Bacon, lettuce, and tomato."

He took a generous bite. "Mm."

"Don't have those in the UK, huh?"

"Um, yes, actually. The abbreviation threw me is all. It's been a while."

"Help yourself." Rose passed him a paper plate and motioned to the rest of the food. "There's something for everyone." She'd gone overboard if she were honest, grabbing snacks from the shelves with abandon, unsure what he'd like. The result was a picnic for five or six people.

"Don't mind if I do." He kept his darkly seductive gaze on her, giving a hidden meaning to his words. "Is this something you do often?" he asked.

"Hardly ever. Why?"

"Just curious."

"About the competition?"

He took a large bite out of his sandwich, waited until he'd stopped chewing before he responded. "I'd rather there wasn't any competition. But if there is, I'm willing to do whatever it takes to be the front runner."

His reply was unexpected and Rose quickly gathered her thoughts. She hardly knew him. A nervous laugh rolled over her lips. "Well, look at you, a go-getter."

"You don't mind me saying that?"

She shrugged, keeping it cool. Inside, she was ready to burst with pride at the intimate attention of the stranger. "Not at all."

Bellamy held up a plastic container filled with a rather expensive delicacy from the gourmet section and studied the contents at close quarters. "A seafood dish?"

"They're pan-seared, hand caught scallops on a bed of baby spinach, finished with bacon sherry vinaigrette. Dig in."

"You're very knowledgeable about cuisine."

"Nah, I'm just reading the label on the side of the container," she replied and gave him a playful wink.

"Well, you pulled it off with culinary brio."

"Yeah? Well, I must be a good actress because I've never had them." Rose picked up a scallop with her thumb and index finger, examining it before tossing it in her mouth. Within seconds, she spat it out and reached for a napkin.

He did nothing to hold back a laugh as she scraped at her tongue with dirty fingernails. "Not quite to your tastes?" Bellamy then leaned across the blanket toward Rose and gently wiped her mouth with a napkin. The motion appeared so minuscule, yet…the nearness of his skin sent hers alight.

"Um, no. I'm not a big seafood fan. I just grabbed it thinking you'd prefer something…fancier," she told him, realizing that there was a little bit of a hidden meaning underneath the statement if he dared look hard enough. What was a guy like Bellamy doing with a girl like her, anyway? They couldn't be more opposite.

He tore his insightful gaze from her face and seemed to hide a grin as his eyes dropped to the spread in front of them. As if he'd read her thoughts and agreed with them.

The silence worked away at Rose while they ate—in her case, nibbled. She'd read somewhere that only ten percent of human communication was verbal. The rest was body language and those almost imperceptible signals sent and received by the most primitive parts of the brain. If a picture was worth a thousand words, one of Bellamy's intense gazes was worth the entire Harlequin catalog. Strangely, the less he said, the clearer she could read him, the closer she felt to uncovering his secrets.

Yes, those darn secrets.

But Rose realized she did trust him, perhaps she had from the beginning, and it scared her a little. She'd done the casual thing before, she'd done inconsequential. Bellamy was neither. This thing they had, whatever it was between them, felt forbidden somehow, not intended. Maybe that was why she wanted it so much, because she wasn't supposed to have it. Wasn't supposed to get involved with a guy so out of tune with the world around them.

Indulging in her dark side was something people had always *assumed* she'd done, but this time they had a point. Bellamy was sweet, but there was also something primal about him. A driving force that didn't yield to gunmen, police, private detectives, or asshole brothers. It was like catnip to Rose. She wanted to see it up close, taste it, feel it inside her. Find that delicate spot where the sweetness became hard and the hardness dissipated to sweet.

She swilled the thought away with a mouthful of Pino Grigio, but the longing persisted. It had a hold of her now. She shrugged her leather jacket off and adjusted her tank top and her bra strap that had become twisted during her near-fall in the boat. Bellamy's gaze explored her shoulders and neck, even dipped into her cleavage. Their eyes met when his lifted from their gaze, and she gave him a devilish glare. B-cups with attitude. Take no prisoners.

The wine went to her head, seeming to cast a misty haze over the intense moment. Rose nearly forgot where she was, but never forgot who she was with. It would take more than Pino to change that. And it was time to quit stalling. Time to make a move. Bellamy's good intentions and old-school ways weren't getting them anywhere.

She emptied her paper cup, dropped it onto her

paper plate, and started to crawl around the picnic toward him.

"I-if you like, there's something I can dip you in," he said, then shook his head, untangling his tongue. "I mean, you can try one of these dips if you like. Barbecue? Cheese and chives?"

Rose grabbed the small container of dip and tossed it aside. "Nope, changed my mind. I have a taste for something else." She spread her knees and straddled him, her breasts level with his face which she grabbed ahold of with her hands. His skin was soft to touch and Rose couldn't help but run her fingers through his gorgeous blonde locks.

Bellamy's chin tipped up towards hers and his eyes widened as she leaned her face closer to his, going in for the kill.

"I, ah…I…" he looked around frantically as if he'd find the proper response just lying there on the ground.

She tilted her head and paused, studying him. "Bellamy, kiss me."

He gulped nervously, but slowly leaned in and kissed her, his dark eyes remaining open and wide with fascination. Those soft pink lips clumsily fumbled with her bright red ones and she giggled at his expense. The man beneath her didn't appear to know what the hell she was doing, but he was clearly enjoying it.

Rose traced a fingernail along his jawline, rasping the overnight stubble. He closed his eyes and took a deep breath, seeming to breathe in the very scent of the moment.

"Bellamy, look at me."

Roused from his daydream, he obeyed, but his eyes were filled with that of a different man. A different…being. Gone was the sweet and vulnerable Bellamy, replaced with a deep, dark intensity that demanded to have her.

"Do whatever you want." She reached behind her back, unfastened her bra and let it fall. "I intend to."

His jaw unhinged. He tried to move, do something, anything, but she clearly had him mesmerized. Like an enchantress over a dark lord.

Rose laughed out loud, a wicked, dirty laugh. "Do you want me, Bellamy?"

His tightening grip on her outer thighs signaled his

response. "You've no idea."

Rose shivered with delight as the gentle breeze crossed her nipples and she shook her head, tossing her hair over her shoulder.

Gasping for oxygen, his gaze skimmed lower, down the length of her pale body. Then, quickly, his eyes darted around the island, searching for something.

"Afraid we'll be caught?" she whispered in his ear.

"No. Just…afraid this might all be a dream."

"Maybe it is." She took his hands and placed them on her body, allowing him permission to do as he pleased. "Show me how the rest of it goes."

He grinned and stared up at her face, their eyes locking and becoming trapped in the intensity that his ignited. "Whatever the lady desires." With a wicked smirk, he toed off his shoes and removed his shirt to reveal his flawless body.

Half-naked, Bellamy grabbed her tightly and pressed her chest up against his warm torso, a place she'd be happy to stay forever. He nuzzled her cheek, and she felt the soft brush of his lips as he whispered in her ear. "Just so you know, Rose, I've seen your dreams, and I know what pleases you."

There wasn't a doubt in her mind. She felt him growing beneath her and Rose gently rolled her hips, eliciting a deep moan from his chest. "Thanks for the heads up."

Rose tingled with excitement from head to toe as she gazed into Bellamy's killer dark brown eyes. All the need and desire that surely filled him shone through his aura of mystery, like sunlight finding its way through the cracks of an old building. The man inside the enigma was ready to catch fire, and she wanted to be his spark. Rose had never felt so alive than right there in that moment. Being with him on this tiny heap of land, away from the world. Nothing else mattered. Bellamy wrapped an arm around her waist so that she couldn't escape even if she'd wanted to. A tiny sigh escaped her throat.

"Rose—"

"Shhh, don't talk." Words hadn't got them this far. Chemistry had. It was time to let that do the talking.

He nodded and traced an index finger along her bottom lip. She nipped the tip, then sucked it in, tonguing the appendage until he groaned.

"Rosssse—" He caught her face, fiercely, in both of

his hands and kissed her with a passion that ignited her insides as nothing had ever done before. No drink. No drug. Nothing in life even seemed real up to this point.

His tongue toyed against the seam of her mouth and she willingly opened to welcome him. He delved in, a beautiful taste of wine and peanut butter touched her taste buds, lapping and swirling until her knees trembled. Hastily, she shifted to remove the rest of her clothes and stood bare before him. Bellamy gawked up at her like someone worshipping a god.

She pointed at his pants. Bellamy didn't take his eyes off hers as he unzipped and released himself–as sight that had her throat running dry.

He grabbed her hand and pulled her back down into his lap and she relished in the warmth of his body. So hot it made her head swim.

With a regretful sigh, she pulled away.

"Did I do something wrong?"

"Nothing. I-I…just need to know this is for real. This craziness. It *feels* like a dream. But…"

His thumb covered her mouth, ordering her to stop. "No, don't think of that now. It's whatever you want it to be, Rose. Delight in it. Delight in me as I will in you."

And so, she did.

Bellamy's powerful hands gripped her naked thighs as he lifted and positioned her just right and their eyes locked as she lowered herself down over the length of him.

She wrapped her arms around his neck as he filled her and their breaths quickened, deepened, and grew warmer between them.

The world melted away. Darkened as if night had fallen up on them and they were all that existed. Rose's knees scraped the earth beneath them as she rocked her body with his, pulling up and then slowly lowering herself back down. Again, and again.

Bellamy's fingers grasped the small of her back, guiding her body, holding her as if he thought she might disappear. All the while, his dark eyes bore into hers, refusing to look away, refusing to even blink. His stare made her shudder, goosebumps scoured her skin. But his warm hands smoothed them away.

As the promise of release began to build, mirroring in Bellamy's tensing body, Rose threw her head back as she quickened each thrust, slamming her body down over his, driving the length of him deeper and deeper insider her.

Bellamy let out a deep moan of pleasure. "Rose…"

She kept her pace, riding out the wave of bliss as she felt his entire body tense and spill his warm release inside her.

"Bellamy…" she breathed over his mouth.

Their shared climax seemed to go on forever, wave after wave, roll after roll. Finally, her body went limp in his arms and all she could do was let him lay her down on the blanket.

She blindly reached for him, her eyes filled with a swirl of darkness and stars, but Bellamy trailed kisses down her still-writhing body until his lips found her center. Boats cruised down the harbor, but Rose didn't care. Let them see, let them wonder in the distance.

She threw her head back and bared her chest to the skies as Bellamy feasted on her.

CHAPTER NINE

"So... what happens now?"

Rose realized it was the first time she'd ever asked that question so soon after making love to a guy for the first time. The question had weight, the answer had consequences, and in her experience men were not comfortable with either, at least not on a first date. But the truth was, neither was she.

The sex had been amazing, far better than she could have hoped for. But now that the silence had returned, reality had begun to seep into their perfect island tryst. Reality in the shape of doubt, bad timing, all the practicalities of hooking up with someone whose life and circumstances she knew precious little about.

A stranger.

He grunted in reply, as though his mind had been wandering and he hadn't heard her the first time.

"Where do we go from here?" she reiterated. "You and me."

After a lengthy pause, "I wish I knew."

"I know it's the worst timing in the world, with my mom like she is..."

"I wish there was something more I could do about that," he replied.

She relaxed her hold on him a tad. They were both still naked, but the breeze was growing persistent; it had cooled her sweat quickly within just a few short minutes, goosing her flesh. "What do you mean— something *more?*"

He let her relax her hold, didn't try to reaffirm his own. "A part of me wants to throw caution to the wind, Rose. Let the chips fall where they may."

"And the rest of you?"

"It's...not as straightforward as that. I'd be lying if I said there wouldn't be consequences to my staying on afterward...with you."

"What's wrong with me?"

"*Nothing*. That's just it," said Bellamy. "You're so right for me, and I don't want to lose sight of you. Just the mere thought of it…"

"Then don't. Stay on." She brushed his tousled blonde hair away from his brow with the backs of her fingers. "Or I could go to you. There's nothing stopping us." But there was. She didn't know what it was, and he wasn't telling her, but sooner or later it was going to hurt. Otherwise he'd have come clean by now.

Bellamy said nothing in reply to her rambling. He seemed to be in a quandary. But she couldn't help him through it if she didn't know the first thing about it.

"You take your work seriously," she said. "I respect that. You don't want to compromise your relationship with your client. I totally get it."

"You do?"

"Uh-huh," she lied. "You feel like you're betraying her trust, going behind her back like this, getting it on with her daughter while she's...you know."

"Partly. But that isn't it."

"Then what is it? You can tell me. Whatever it is, I'll

understand."

He snatched a glance at her out of the corner of his eye, then gazed skyward through the swaying branches, the sighing leaves. "I don't think you *can* understand. Even *I* don't fully understand it all."

Rose had to dig deep into her investigative bag of tricks. She was so close to his secret, to him wanting to tell her, all she had to do was find his pressure point, the right question to draw the truth out. He might be the cagiest customer she'd ever dealt with but his cage was not as strong as he'd let on. Tossing her clues and riddles through the bars was only making her more determined to pick the lock. Hell, to break the damn door down if she had to, if it meant keeping Bellamy in her life. Her mom had brought him into their world; surely, she wouldn't be against him staying on.

"Try me," she pleaded. "Unless you're on the run for some sort of capital crime, I've been known to help people out of all sorts of tight corners." She waited for a response, didn't get one, so she tried another tack. "So, you're not married, you're not wanted for a capital crime, and your name isn't Max de Winter. What else? No incurable diseases? You're not liable to spontaneously combust?"

"We very nearly *did*. Twice." He cleared his throat and Rose warmed inside at the sudden redness that spread through his cheeks.

"True. But I'm running out of reasons for us not to give this a go. You know, to see where it leads us. I know we literally just met, but I can't see how we could just part ways when this is all over."

"Rose, your mother will—"

"I know, I know. My mom will have to tell me when the time is right." The distant sound of laughter made her sit up. Somebody was approaching on the water. "But what if she doesn't get the chance? Would you ever tell me, after she's gone, or would that violate your NDA?" That last part came out with more vitriol than she'd intended.

"If your mother doesn't tell you, I swear I will."

"Fair enough. In the meantime," She rushed to gather her clothes, then tossed him his, "we keep this between us, what happened today, I mean."

"Agreed. But I'd like to take you to dinner," he added. "Would that be okay?"

"Ah, yeah, I guess." It was the quickest Rose had ever gotten dressed. The kayakers were almost at the beach. She could discern the individual voices; two giggly young women, maybe teenagers, and a slightly older guy. "I'll go on one condition," she said.

"What's that?"

"That you tell me how you knew that mugger yesterday."

Bellamy shrugged as he zipped up his khakis. The guy sure wasn't in a hurry to cover up; he didn't even have his shirt on yet. "We crossed paths a few years back. He'd shot a woman. But instead of fleeing, he stayed at the scene, tried to make it look like someone else had done it. The problem was, he hadn't killed her right away. She was still alive when the sirens approached."

"So, he finished her off?"

"No. He didn't know she was still alive. But she was watching him the whole time. Watching, hating, praying to be saved, praying for justice."

"So, she identified him to the cops?"

"Unfortunately, no. She died before the paramedics got there."

"Wait a minute. Where do *you* fit in in all this? How do you know she was watching him and praying?"

"Because I was there."

"You witnessed it?"

He nodded, and at the same time hit her with a fierce, almost primal look that seemed to warn her: *I saw it all, and believe me, you never want to see anything like that.*

"Well, I wouldn't have tried to tangle with a gun-wielding psycho either," she replied feebly. Then it hit her. "But that didn't stop you yesterday. You walked up to him unarmed, no hesitation. Bellamy, he could have *shot* you."

"But he didn't."

"And you were certain he wouldn't?"

"Certain enough."

"But how?" she asked, frantically grabbing for answers.

Carefully tucking his polo shirt into his shorts, he gave an even more careful reply. "Because the first time we met, I told him something I knew he'd never forget."

"Really? What was that?"

He heaved a deep sigh. "I told him how he was going to die."

***

On the bus home, Bellamy offered her his hand. She hesitated, his words still ringing in her ears.

I told him how he was going to die.

But she quickly shook the unease away and slipped her fingers into his grasp where they happily stayed the entire ride home. Being with him was a strange kind of unpredictable. It could be thrilling; their rooftop rendezvous, the unexpected kiss in the street, the boat ride to the island, the super hot sex. But every so often the unpredictability became a little scary, as though events were dangerously out of her control; his intervention with the mugger, the way he talked his way around the police, his unfathomable liaison with her mom.

Rose felt either extraordinarily lucid around him or unable to form a coherent thought or memory. It was bizarre. Everything on the way to the island, and all that had happened *on* it was indelible in her mind.

Unforgettable. Yet, leaving the island and everything since was a blur. Almost as though it had happened to someone else and she'd kind of, sort of, observed without really paying attention.

I told him how he was going to die.

What on earth did Bellamy mean by that? That he'd someday actually get even with the gunman, make him pay for killing that woman? Or had it just been an empty threat, a macho rush of blood covering for the fact that Bellamy had witnessed the murder but hadn't been able to stop it? The more she wrung the words through her mind, together with everything else she knew about him, the more convinced she became that this man she'd fallen for was not beholden to the same rules, the same laws as ordinary people.

But which government agency did he work for? In what capacity? An independent contractor perhaps? Some kind of shadowy facilitator with international ties? Her mom had found him, though, and hired him.

Or had he found her?

Rose's dad had left her mom a small fortune in the divorce. Was she planning to do something crazy with it, and Bellamy was helping her make it happen?

Whatever his deal was, it scared Rose to death. And that was a bitter aftertaste to what had been such a delicious date on the island. It suddenly left her distrustful of him, her mom, and everyone else involved. It made her want to go back to her apartment in the city, bury her head in a mountain of work. Come back when she could be alone with her mom. No mystery men, no jerk brother, just the two of them talking about stuff and working the world out over a bottle of wine and a bag of chips.

All these men and their bullshit.

If only all men could just screw off and leave her and her mom alone. If only she could shake loose of him. If only she could stand the idea of things going back to the way they were before he'd stirred these feelings inside her. These feelings, fresh and warm, she knew wouldn't go away anytime soon.

***

Andy and another young man, a little gormless-looking and sporting a varsity t-shirt, were leaving the building as Rose returned. They looked sullen. Andy looked hard at her, then at Bellamy, but said nothing. The other guy held the door for her, smiled politely when she thanked him.

It might be a sunny day but a shadow hung over it now. One that chilled her heart, as though bad news had been piling up all around her and she'd been oblivious to its approach; its arrival was imminent, yet she was going to be the last to know. Andy knew it, Bellamy knew it, her mom knew it. Hell, even the varsity guy probably knew it.

"Do me a favor." Propping the door open, she reached into her purse and plucked out a ratty looking twenty-dollar bill and handed it to Bellamy. "There's a grocery store about three blocks that way." She nodded up the street. "Grab us some drinks? My feet are killing me from all that walking, but I could murder a cold beer."

He cast her a suspicious look. "Any preference?"

"Not really. As long as it's ice-cold, I'm all over it. Get some for yourself, too."

He shrugged and leaned in to plant a delicate and reserved kiss on her cheek. "Very well."

She fought the urge to pull him into her, to make the kiss last longer. "Cool. Don't be long."

But she knew he would be. The store was more like five blocks and two side streets away. Plenty of scope for him to get lost; plenty of time for her to have a word with her mom. The second the main building door closed behind her, Rose bolted up the stairs.

"You kids have fun?" Blythe slid her glasses to the end of her nose, saw that Rose was alone as she barreled in through the door. Her mom put down the magazine she'd been reading. "Let me guess. He fell down a manhole?"

"Ah, you could say that, sort of."

"Oh. A hole of his own making, then." The way her mom narrowed her eyes, just a fraction, with a slight tilt of her head, was a sure tell-tale sign that she was on top of this meeting, of what would go unsaid between them. She'd always been sharp and intuitive, maybe the sharpest person Rose had ever met. Little escaped her attention. "You've been gone a while."

"We took a trip to the harbor."

"You went to the harbor-front? The Halifax side?"

"Yeah, took a little boat out to one of the small

islands. Had it pretty much to ourselves."

"You sound a little flustered, Rose."

"Nah, just tired." Rose plonked herself down on the sofa, put her dirty sneakers up on the coffee table. "Yeah, just tired...of all the cloak and dagger shit around here."

"Excuse me? And take your shoes off my table."

"Uh-huh." Her mom was literally the only person in the world Rose would have obeyed in her current frame of mind. It stung her a little to be at odds like this, but she really *was* tired of being excluded from whatever was going on.

"By cloak and dagger, you mean..."

"You know exactly what I mean. Shit, you've even told Andy before me."

Blythe took her glasses off, folded them slowly, and placed them neatly in their case. "What did he tell you?"

"Enough to know you and Bellamy are playing me for a first-class sucker." She was lying, grasping at straws, but she was desperate.

"In other words, he told you nothing," Blythe replied.

"Not nothing. I know my brother. I know when he's covering for someone."

"Rose, you need to work on your bluffing technique. That was feeble."

"I know. Like I said, I'm tired." Rose scrubbed her face with her hands. "I came here to spend time with you, and it feels like all I've been doing is figuring out why you don't want me here."

Blythe shook her head and gave a long, weary sigh. "You poor girl. You couldn't be further from the truth. Rose, this has *all* been about spending more time with you. If you believe anything, believe that. Trust me. Bellamy wouldn't hear otherwise."

Rose sat up. "Mom, what does that even *mean?* What are you saying?"

"I'm saying...I've said too much. He's not who you think he is, Rose. I just need you to be careful."

"And if I'm not?"

"Then I don't know what will happen."

"Does anyone?" asked Rose. "Did you, when you fell for what-was-his-name? Hank?"

"So, you *have* fallen for him?" Blythe slowly folded her arms, looked across to a photo on the mantel—

one of her favorites. It was of them both together. "Tell me, who pursued who?"

Rose didn't reply. Neither the answer nor the purpose of the question were clear to her. She felt cornered. Ready to snap. And the last thing she wanted to do was fight her mom. The time they had was too precious to be doing that.

"Never mind," Blythe continued with a fidgety manner. "I'm sure you know what you're doing."

An awkward silence suffocated the air between them. They avoided eye contact until it became almost unbearable for Rose.

"Who was that with Andy?" Rose asked. "The goofy looking guy I saw downstairs."

"Oh, Kurt. Andy's roommate. They're watching a monster truck show or something tonight. Seems like a nice boy. Polite. Parents are from Newfoundland." Blythe paused to sip her tea. "But just for tonight. He's heading back to the city tomorrow."

"Good, this weekend is supposed to be spent with you," Rose replied and then cringed when she thought of how she was gone all day.

"Tomorrow I thought we could take a trip

together—you, me, Andy...and Bellamy."

"What sort of a trip?"

"A trip down memory lane. Andy's promised to drive us."

"Really? You feel up to a road trip? Where to? What if you need to lie down or something?"

"I'll be fine. It's important to me that we go, and that we go together, as a family. Do you mind?"

Rose got up and slouched onto the arm of her mom's chair, hugging her with one arm. It was her way of saying, *I don't know what you're up to, Mom, but I'm with you, wherever you want to go.*

Her mother gave her a gentle pat on the arm. "Thanks, sweetie."

"What if Bellamy doesn't want to go?" asked Rose.

"You leave him to me." Gone was the softness from her mom's voice. Instead, she sounded almost defiant. "I'll ask him in such a way that he won't be able to say no."

"Or I could ask him," Rose suggested. "It sounds like you're giving him some kind of ultimatum."

"I wouldn't put it that strongly."

"But I thought you two were—"

"We have a contract. But he isn't family. And I can't pretend I'm happy with his conduct."

"I see. And you don't approve of me and him…"

Blythe said nothing and Rose knew she would get nothing further form her mother. So, instead, she let the quiet hum of the room surround them and rested her head atop her mother's. Her hand slid down to spread across Blythe's chest where she could feel her mother's heart. It was a rhythm that never lied. It was the rhythm of life. Of love.

But what about death?

Surely, death must have a rhythm of its own?

***

"Bellamy, come sit with me."

It was a little under an hour to midnight. Rose was asleep in her room. The traffic outside had eased to a trickle, but in Blythe's mind, a tornado surrounded her. A silent wrecking swirl of emotion that had been brewing for hours, ever since Rose had all-but-admitted her feelings for their deathly chaperon.

He sat on the sofa, not in his usual spot directly

opposite her but on the side farthest away. Subtle maybe, but it was the first acknowledgment she'd seen from him that things were not as they should be. That something about their bargain had been altered.

Blythe nodded his attention to the wall clock. "I don't think I need to point it out, but I'm going to anyway. Our deal was for three days. Three extra days. We're now in the final day. By tomorrow night, we'll both be gone."

He stayed silent. Didn't look at the clock or her. The photo on the mantel distracted him, as it had on their first meeting. She hadn't known why at the time, but she'd noticed his preoccupation with it nonetheless. Over the past two days, the reason had become all too clear.

"Why?" she asked.

"Why what?"

"Don't play games with me. You entered into a bargain, but you did it under false pretenses."

He sat up straight, ready to battle it out. "Explain."

"Gladly. You fancied my daughter the second you laid eyes on her picture. From then on, everything you've said and done has been motivated by one thing: to get close to her." She waved away his protest. "Don't try to deny it. This was never about me getting to spend more time with her; it was about *you*. You and her. By this time tomorrow night, I'll be out of her life forever and it'll break her heart. But at least it's natural. It's the way things eventually had to go. That much I can take."

She paused to take a deep breath. "But *you!* You're in a whole new world of cruelty. What started out as me saying goodbye to my little girl has turned into this twisted, toxic thing between us. Her and I used to be so close. We used to be able to tell each other anything. But ever since you came on the scene we've been tying each other in knots trying to pretend you're not here, that you don't matter, like some dark sheet of glass between us."

Blythe let those words sit with him. If he truly cared for Rose, surely he must see what he's doing to her. What will happen to her once the two of them are gone?

"In the meantime, you're inching closer into her confidence, getting to know what she likes, keeping her off guard. When you break my baby's world apart, know that you've got an eternity of hurt heading your way, because I'll haunt you to the end of days."

"So, I should take something to read, then," he replied cheekily and snatched up the Steven Pressfield novel she was currently reading. "Gates of Fire. How apt. No wonder you're in a foul mood."

She snatched it back from him, noticing how creased the spine was—she'd read it several times over the years, had always had the same strong ambivalent reaction to its Spartan heroes. Hate and admiration. She hated how they lived, what they stood for; but she admired their passion, conviction, and their refusal to bow to any foreign rule. Before she knew it, those three virtues had rushed to her head. She drew back her arm and hurled her paperback into the face of Death.

Luckily for both of them, he ducked.

"So that's how you taught history," he said. "Your Bible class must have been especially painful."

"Don't get cute with me. Either you explain to me right now what you hope to get from seducing my daughter, or I blow a hole right through our bargain."

"Hmm. I'm getting a little tired of these threats, Blythe."

"Oh? How about now?" From under the cushion at her side, she retrieved a small handgun, her husband's ultimate means of home protection he'd thankfully never had to use. Neither had she. Until now. She pointed it at the center of his chest.

He glowered back at her, the dark blaze in his eyes far more intense than the glow of the reading lamp, the only source of light in the room. "Maybe I misjudged you," he spoke carefully. "I didn't take you for a murderer."

"You're already dead. I'm just putting you out of our misery, mine and Rose's, that is."

"But she's falling in love with me, Blythe."

She guffawed. "It's only been two days."

Bellamy only offered a casual shrug.

"No. She loves the *idea* of you." She shook her head. "You don't even exist."

"And neither will you if you pull that trigger. To her, you'll have murdered the man she thinks she's falling for. The first man she's ever felt anything for. With your final gesture, you'll destroy her memory of you. I really don't think that's how you want to be remembered by your beloved, as a killer."

"That's precious, coming from a grim reaper."

He cocked his head slightly to one side, then, with his fingers, combed his long hair back behind his ears. "Then do it. I'm not going to stop you. I could, you know—as easily as snuffing out a candle—but I'm not going to. Be it on your own soul, Blythe Foley, and prepare to reap the consequences of your wrath."

She thought over what he'd said, knew he was right. Rose was confused enough already. Adding a murder to the mix would not only destroy her emotionally, but it might also rob her of the answers to all the riddles. But Blythe had never intended to shoot Bellamy—only to threaten it. No, she had a much simpler solution in mind.

"You're right. I can't kill you," she said, then pressed the muzzle to her own temple. "But *this* would ruin things for you."

He jerked forward a few inches. His intense glower softened, quivered at the edges, betraying the fear inside. "You wouldn't."

"Then talk."

He swallowed. "You're not bluffing."

Blythe clicked the hammer. "No."

"Then why would you—"

"To save Rose from you. I told you once before I'll do anything to protect my children. *Anything.* Are we clear?"

"What is it you want to know?" he asked.

"Everything. I want to know what your plan is after the three days are up. I want to know what you have in mind for my daughter. How long are you going to stay in this human form? Are you going to try to take her with you?" Tears escaped her stone demeanor at the last question.

For the first time, he couldn't hold his gaze on her. He looked down at the carpet instead and sighed in defeat.

"You don't know *what* you're doing, do you?" she concluded. "You're making this up as you go. It's not what you're supposed to be doing at all."

"How did you know?"

"It's written all over you, Bellamy. You might be an all-powerful force of the universe when you're invisible, but you're center stage now, and you're improvising. You were smitten with Rose and now you're improvising a last act love story." Blythe lowered the gun, feeling bad for the man in front of her. "The problem is, dear, you weren't hired to play a love story. You're the cloaked figure who carries a scythe and ends all love stories. You're here to take me away. The longer you stay, the worse it gets. The more painful it becomes for everyone involved. You can't take Rose with you without killing her. You can't stay without messing up the natural order of the universe. And you know I mean every one of my threats. Wherever I go, I'll never rest until you pay for ruining my daughter's future and breaking her heart. So, what's the deal, Bellamy? You want to stick to the script, or do *you* want to reap the consequences of *my* wrath?" She lifted the unloaded weapon again, pressed it against her forehead. "Decide now."

He lunged forward with an outstretched arm, stopped short, and balled his fist in frustration. "You win, Blythe. Don't pull that trigger. Whatever you do, don't destroy this for me. For Rose."

"So, you *do* think it can work out. You think there can be a happy-ever-after."

"I—I don't know." His broad shoulders slumped.

"Not a good answer."

"I *hope* there can be a way," he admitted. "I feel like there can be. It's…it's hard to explain."

"Try me."

As he sank back into the sofa, Bellamy's entire being seemed to relax. He was no longer stiff, poised. He was the young man whose form he'd taken, the laid-back, carefree youth from her past, come to life. The son she might have had, if her life unfolded differently. Hank Bonden's son. It was no longer Death sitting opposite her; it was the man before death, the long-lost soul from another epoch, hoping beyond hope that he might finally get to live out the life that Fate had previously denied him. To fall in love and be loved in return, unconditionally. To have a family if he wanted, or didn't. To make new mistakes and form new regrets, and use centuries of secondhand experience to make Rose as happy as he possibly could for the rest of her life.

If even half of that was true, she couldn't blame him for wanting to find a way.

She lowered the gun once more and sighed. "I think

it's time you let me help you, Bellamy. Whatever crisis you're in, maybe we can find a way through it. For Rose."

"In that case," he said, "first I need to tell you about an unusual rendezvous I had recently. One that threw me off my game."

"By rendezvous, you mean you were summoned to help someone pass on?"

"Yes. But this one was different. I felt it was going to be different before I even met her, just like I can feel now that things can't go back to the way they were. *I* can't go back to that, to the way I was. Encountering Rose was no fluke. I can't explain why, but it all started with that rendezvous. Samantha Byers was her name. She was seventy-seven years old when I came to collect her. Even before I met her, I could tell there was a touch of destiny about the woman. She knew things, things I couldn't see."

"Like what?" Blythe spoke aloud without realizing it. Her eagerness to finally know the truth about her dark chaperon had her perched on the edge of her favorite chair. "Sorry. Go on."

"A premonition. Samantha could see ahead to a

crucial moment in her daughter's life, hours into the future after Samantha's death. I didn't believe her at first because *I* couldn't see it, and if someone with my insight couldn't see ahead then how could she, a mere mortal?"

Bellamy paused to flex his taut fingers.

"But she convinced me to let her linger a while after her death, to make sure her vision came to pass. It was important for her daughter's happiness. Then something happened that I've never experienced in all the time I've been doing this. To avert a disaster, Samantha reached out from the in-between, *back* into the world of the living, to warn her daughter away from danger. She spoke to her *and* touched her. I didn't know how at the time. She later suggested that I must have lent her that power momentarily, without realizing it. The scenario did have uncanny echoes of my own life at the time of my death. And I did *want* her daughter to survive, to have her happy ending. Either way, Samantha's prophecy came true against impossible odds. Yet, it wouldn't have if she and I hadn't intervened to save her daughter's life at the last second."

Blythe let the comfortable silence hang between them. No reply of hers could help the pain wrought across Bellamy's face at the memories.

"I learned two important lessons from that rendezvous. The first was that I know only a small part of the workings of Destiny. I have a role to play in helping souls pass on to the Great Beyond, but I also have the ability to improvise in ways I hadn't realized before. To alter the lives of the living. I'm neither alive nor a part of the Great Beyond. I'm something else. And the longer I remain as master of the in-between, the more alone I truly feel."

He sighed.

"There isn't much I remember about my life before death. It's another one of the countless lives I've observed and come to understand during my strange journey. But recently, during my meeting with Samantha, and now with you and Rose, I'm reminded of the things I had once and lost, those things that were snatched from me: a family, a future, a wife who loved me. I remember the things I felt, and how strongly I felt them. Being with Rose has brought the past to life in ways you can't imagine. Past naturally precedes the future; the two go hand in hand. And the clearer the one, the clearer the other, at least that's what I've found these past few days.

She opened her mouth to speak but he continued hastily. Leaning forward and touching his hand to his chest. Over his heart.

"I'm changed, Blythe. I can no longer be an observer. I'm a part of the world again. I'm part of Rose's world. If that means I must renounce my calling, then I'm willing to do whatever it takes. I don't even know if it's possible. All I know is that my encounter with Samantha spun my destiny off its course. It sent me to you and, thankfully, to Rose."

Blythe shuffled uncomfortably on her cushion. His story stirred intrigue, even excitement—he was talking about defying the laws of the universe, for God's sake—but in the middle of it all was Rose, sweet, troubled Rose, ready to rush headlong into the least promising relationship in the history of the world. A forbidden romance straight out of Greek tragedy, the stakes beyond comprehension.

"That's either the most recklessly irresponsible thing I've ever heard," she told him, "or you've just made a believer out of me."

"I don't have any answers, Blythe. I can't tell you how or even if it can work out between Rose and I. All I can tell you is that I must try."

"Are you going to tell all this to Rose?"

He hesitated, nervously wiped his palms on his pants. Was Death sweating? *Was* he even that same entity anymore? Or was he now more man than reaper?

Then it hit her. No, more like infected her thoughts while she considered everything that had happened and everything he'd said these past few days. This was all uncharted territory. But what if this "touch of destiny" he'd mentioned was more obvious than he realized? What if the answer was right in front of him? What if his time had indeed come, and Fate *had* led him here for the very things he was agonizing over?

"We're taking a road trip tomorrow," she said. "I think you should come."

The idea seemed to snap him out of his troubled mind. "Where are we going?"

Blythe grinned. "To see an old friend."

"Who?"

"Someone you haven't met. But he'll recognize you all the same."

Bellamy grinned. "And you said *I* speak in riddles." He sprouted a cute, lopsided grin that reminded her of how young he truly was, or how young the man whose form he'd taken had been when he'd died in the fire all those years ago. "It must be important," he added.

"It is. I think it's part of why you're here. I'm starting to think this was all meant to be."

"The touch of destiny?" he mused.

"If it's true that everything happens for a reason, then it's going to happen whether we want it to or not, right?"

Bellamy shrugged. "I suppose."

"Then we've got a day to find out where this path leads. Let's make it count."

"And if we don't find our answer by tomorrow night?" he asked.

"I don't know. But if it's not looking good, promise me one thing."

"What's that?"

Blythe folded her hands in her lap. "That you won't break Rose's heart. Whatever it takes, you'll find a way to make her forget that you ever existed."

"I promise, I'll do everything in my power to not break her heart."

"Whatever it takes?"

He held up a hand like a boy scout. "As God is my witness."

Blythe pointed a stern finger at him. "Good. That's good. Now, where were we?" She rummaged around in the bag hanging from the stand next to her chair and retrieved a deck of cards. "Crazy eights. Your deal."

He erected the small, fold-away wooden table they'd used last night and stood it between them. "What say we up the stakes?"

"Okay. Five years a hand?"

"Five *minutes*, yes." He shook his head. "Years, huh? I'm going to miss you, Blythe."

"Me too, Bellamy. I mean that. Whatever happens, I'm glad it was you."

He shuffled expertly, dealt the cards like a pro. Then he gave an uncharacteristically huge sigh as he lifted his own hand of cards to his face. "Here we go."

CHAPTER TEN

Crammed in the back of Andy's souped-up red Camaro wasn't exactly the most comfortable place to be during a three-and-a-half-hour road trip, but Rose wasn't complaining. She had Bellamy with her on the back seat. When they weren't holding hands or she wasn't nestling her head on his shoulder, he was swiveling this way and that, trying to take in as much as he could of the Nova Scotia countryside, its truck-stops, roadside diners, farms, and pretty much anything they came across. Honestly, the guy was the most unworldly person she'd ever met.

He knew all about people, history, how the world worked, but he seemed to have experienced almost none of it. Like some cloistered scholar allowed out in the wide world for the weekend, he was happier than a child on his birthday.

And Rose loved watching him marvel at everything she took for granted. It made her feel young and mature at the same time. Protective. Optimistic. It would never get old, this feeling, as long as he was this sweet and out-of-sync with the twenty-first century.

Blythe, in the passenger seat, didn't say much. But Rose could tell her mom enjoyed listening to Andy prattle on next to her, filling her in on what he'd been up to. She'd cast him a slightly bemused, fully adoring look now and then, as if to say, *I haven't a clue what you're talking about but I wouldn't miss it for the world.*

Even Rose sort of warmed to the little jerk's openness after a while. He left nothing out; where his buddies were from, their prospects, screw-ups, family histories, the pros and cons of letting them hang out with him. He barely paused for breath whenever he got going. But there was always a wry, knowing humor behind that slightly superior, self-aggrandizing way he had of telling a story. It made him an engaging raconteur. As much as she hated to admit it, Rose could see why he was so popular at college, why people of both sexes gravitated toward him.

Andy was the opposite of Rose. Open and friendly where she was snarky and closed off. He went out of his way to dress well, have perfect hair, and to be fashionable; she dressed however the hell she felt like that morning, had only ever had good hair days accidentally, and generally loathed fashion trends. He had a queue of people his age wanting to hang out with him, while Rose seemed to cause a social stampede in the opposite direction whenever she opened her mouth or cast a glance in any direction.

But all of that was okay because she had a man in her life. A man who, like her, had almost nothing in common with her brother. A man who made her feel a little less like a social reject because he was further off than she.

"...really into Sue Wetherall, but she has a thing for Italian guys. It's the weirdest study group on campus 'cause there's all this tension, like a four-way unrequited thing going on. Me and Kurt only show up when we have to, otherwise, we'd have to hold some sort of intervention for those poor saps, get them to finally come clean with each other before their heads explode."

"Sounds like a tangled web," Blythe replied, humoring him. "Who's this girl you've been seeing again?"

"Which one?"

Rose rolled her eyes at Bellamy and he gave her a little wink.

"The one you were telling us about," her mom went on. "The advanced robotics girl."

"Cheryl. Yeah, she invited me up to P.E.I to meet her folks." Andy then paused, seemingly unsure if he should have said that. "But…I told her it wasn't a good time right now."

Blythe's drooped with sadness. "On account of me?"

"Of course. I've only got one mom."

He'd never said a sweeter thing in his life. Rose couldn't see, but she guessed her mom would be tearing up right now. Even if he didn't give her another kind word, she'd always be glad he'd said that.

"Wait a minute. I think I recognize this place." Rose

pointed out a long, gently rising country road lined with dandelions, winding through farmland toward a small town ringed by a thick green forest. The road they were on forked ahead, giving them access. "It's been ages, but that town—we stayed there once, right? Or…somewhere near it at least?"

"I wasn't sure you'd remember," Blythe answered with a proud grin. "What about you, Andy?"

"Um, nope. Not a clue. What's it called?"

"Greenwood."

"Sounds fake," he replied.

"Greenwood?" Rose turned the name over a few times in her mind. "I remember something about a hospital. And police cars. The name definitely rings a bell."

"Take a left," Blythe told Andy. "I'll guide you to it."

"I can *see* the town, Mom," he replied with residual teenage angst.

"We're not going to the town...yet."

"Then where?" Andy replied.

Their mother hugged herself as she peered longingly out the window. "Just wait."

Andy gripped the steering wheel as the sun blared in

through all the windows. "Mom, you're freaking me out. There's nothing else out here."

"Maybe not anymore. But there was once."

"It'd better be worth it. I'm missing day two of monster trucks for this."

Blythe said nothing. She just ignored the world inside the car and focused on the one outside, or the one in her mind as she wistfully stared off in the distance.

The spot she picked out for them to stop at, about a quarter-mile up a well-used dirt road, was in a clearing inside a spindly offshoot of the forest. They all stepped out of the vehicle and glanced around the old property. The tree line which surrounded the property was thinning from years of neglect. The space was flat and bare, about the size of a city block. It had been trampled so much, for so long that no new grass grew from the claylike topsoil. Part of it was even scorched black. A large gravelly area in the center appeared to have been shaped into a kind of distended ellipse, with a semicircular space joined onto one end. An old vending hut with the sign still intact—Greenwood Valley Fair Snacks—Hot Dogs,

Burgers, Fries—stood on the edge of the semicircle. Other clues as to the site's former identity included a large rusted trailer with flat tires, pieces of torn canopy festooning the lower branches of overgrown trees, partially torn flyers ground into the dirt, and a few coils of metal cable left on the gravel.

Rose closed her eyes, tried to imagine the dimensions of the place when it had thrived with people and attractions and life. The sights, sounds, especially the smells. Cotton candy. Hot dogs. Bundles of fresh hay.

"This was it," she said to her mom. "This was where the fire happened. The fire at the fair. I remember."

"What do you remember?"

"Screaming. Crying. But someone was laughing, too. One of those really infectious laughs. I remember thinking about how disturbing it was. It couldn't have been real, could it?"

"I wouldn't have thought so. Andy? I know you were only young. Do you remember any of this?"

He looked up from his cell phone, gazed around at some length, then shrugged. "I dunno. There's something familiar about this place. Can't put my finger on it, though. Don't know anything about a fire. What's the deal, Mom?"

So, Blythe explained what had happened, who they were with that day—Dad's friend and his older son—but she left out the part where she'd been seeing Hank Bonden behind Dad's back. Rose couldn't find it in her to blame anyone for that affair. Mom and Dad had never been close. She'd always felt that. And knowing what had happened in college, how they'd first met, the crossed wires, thwarted desires and such, left Rose oddly ambivalent about the whole thing.

What would I have done in her place?

"Don't know who that is," Andy admitted, referring to the Bondens. "Something about that crazy laugh, though." He turned to Rose. "Wasn't it one of those laughing dummies you get at fairs and circuses and stuff? You know, the super creepy ones that give you nightmares?"

"Yes. That's it!" Rose pointed above them. "It was up over the entrance to the big tent—the big top— laughing down at us. All the while the fire was burning, that stupid thing was laughing at us. Even during the horrible screams. Then it suddenly stopped. I remember thinking later that I hoped the fire had melted its face. I blamed the clown for the whole thing." Rose looked to her mother and frowned. "Hank's son didn't come back, but you told me he'd gotten out, that he'd gone home with friends, but I didn't believe you. I had a suspicion he was the boy that got burned. That was the last time I saw him, and I guess the last time I saw Hank."

Blythe slowly nodded her lament. During the silence that followed, Bellamy wandered off to explore the site. The scorched earth and gravel were the only evidence that the tragic event had ever taken place. Blythe made her way over to Rose and whispered, motioning to Bellamy, "Who does he remind you of?"

Rose shrugged.

"That night was a turning point in our lives," explained Blythe. "Thomas Bonden wasn't the only casualty of the fire, you know."

"I don't know anything. I realize that now. Neither of us does," she replied, referring to Andy, who was chatting on his cell, oblivious to everything.

"Hank was injured too. Badly. They rushed him to the hospital. I wanted to go with him but I couldn't leave the two of you, so I had no choice but to wait. I called Sylvia and Roy, our old neighbors—you remember them? Anyway, they came as soon as they could, to look after you while I went to see about Hank, but before they got here I felt this sharp pain ripping through my arm and my shoulder. I couldn't stop it. It was a heart attack—a full-on myocardial infarction."

Rose felt like the life had hastily been sucked from her body, leaving nothing behind but doubt and endless questions. "So *that's* what brought that on? Now it makes sense. More sense than stress at work, anyway."

Blythe grabbed her hand and held it tightly before lifting to her lips. "I know. I'm sorry I lied to you, Rose. It's just that...I tried to put that night behind me, out of my mind for good. It was too painful to relive it, not just because of the heart attack, but because it snatched Hank away from me for good and his pain of losing Thomas...I just couldn't bear it. I was selfish."

"He didn't die, did he? I thought you said—"

"No, he didn't die. But he was never the same again."

"What happened?"

Blythe put a hand on her daughter's shoulder. "First I want you to look at him—look really hard."

Again, she drew Rose's attention to Bellamy.

"Okay. This is getting weird, Mom."

"I know, but I need you to think. To remember. Who does he remind you of? Where have you seen him before?"

"You're not making any sense. If I'd met him before, I'd have recognized him by now. Wouldn't I?" But she looked hard anyway, more admiringly than ever. He was in his late twenties, boyishly handsome but unselfconscious with it. His long blond hair did seem like a bit of a throwback to a different era—the seventies maybe—but it suited him. There was a lapsed biker thing happening in his appearance, until you got to know him...

An image flashed through her mind. It was him, or seemed to be him, only he was dressed differently.

Sunday best. Her memory kicked in like a movie as she recalled bits and pieces of this alternate Bellamy. He slouched, smoked a cigarette when he thought no one was watching. A group of teenage girls wearing hot pants and tight tees waved to him, giggled when he waved back. He grinned when they left, looked almost smug.

Little Rose had been jealous. But when she caught his eye, and he knew he'd been seen smoking and flirting, he tossed her a wink. She recalled blushing and swelled with pride that an older boy had paid attention to her. He was the best-looking guy she'd ever seen, and though he was way too old for her—she was still a child, waiting out the summer before she entered junior high—but he'd let her in on his secret.

She snapped back to the present, shivered. "Okay, this is getting weirder by the minute." She took her mom by the arm. "Who does he remind me of? Where do *you* think I've seen him before?"

"So, you do recognize him?"

"Yes," Rose then cast a look over her shoulder to Bellamy who was lurking in the thin tree line, touching the leaves and lifting them to his nose, "But it's…it's impossible. I was just a kid, but he still looks…" She shook her head to toss away the thought.

Her mom kissed her on the cheek and patted her arm.

"You're not going to tell me, are you?" she stated.

"We've got one more stop to make. Then I promise you'll have all your answers. I needed you to come back here, though. Like I said, this is where everything changed. None of us were the same after that night."

Rose heaved a heavy sigh and flapped her arms at her sides. "Then let's go. You're making me feel like the worst PI in the world."

"Not the worst, far from it," her mom insisted. "But maybe the unluckiest…"

Another piece in a long line of cryptic clues that Blythe and Bellamy had fed her over the past few days. But if it meant she was about to find out the truth behind this rapidly expanding mystery, she could handle being in the blind for one more ride.

It was going to be the ride of their lives.

CHAPTER ELEVEN

A faded, lime green iron door didn't match anything about the otherwise ordinary-looking old farmhouse. Instead of wooden steps, a long, shallow ramp led up to the porch, flanked by white railings. Rusty farm vehicles rested around a disused concrete yard away to the left. The stables appeared empty as did the doorless barn. There was no car parked outside the house and no one answered the doorbell. Rose even knocked on the horrid iron door a few times, the paint chipping away under her knuckles, but got no reply.

"Whoever it is, they're not home," she concluded.

"Maybe. But not necessarily." Blythe waved her daughter aside, twisted the knob, and pressed on the heavy door. It groaned open on its old hinges, making a noise similar to a waking giant. Her mother stepped inside and called out, "Hello? Hank? It's Blythe. Are you home?"

At first, she received no reply. Rose noted how clutter-free the hall and the adjoining rooms were. One could walk from the front door straight through to the back of the house without a single obstacle in the way. But that wasn't all. Handrails along the walls suggested the occupant was unwell, maybe had trouble walking. Yet, there was no stair-lift of any kind.

Footsteps on the landing drew everyone's attention to the stairs. In a nervous jitter of movements, Blythe corralled Rose and the boys to one side, saying, "You'll want to give him some room."

Rose tried casting her mind back to that day at the fair, to before the fire. She'd spent time with this man, maybe on more than one occasion. Why couldn't she picture him? His face was a blur in the chaos of otherwise sharp images.

"I heard voices. Who's there?" came the shout from aloft. Not an alarmed call, but more a playfully curious one.

"Hank... I–it's Blythe." When he didn't respond, she added, "Told you I'd come."

"Blythe?" Tenderness and disbelief rang in the voice. "How did you...I thought you were sick."

"Not as sick as we thought, apparently. Still had enough go in me for one more trip." Careful steps began to shuffle down the long staircase and Rose could see the nervous way her mother wrung her fingers.

"You should've called. I'd have gotten Steph to set up something special for supper."

"Don't you worry about that, now," she replied. "Is Steph around?"

"It's her afternoon off." Hank finally descended the stairs enough for them to see him, and stopped about halfway down. "Who's that with you?" Hank Bonden was leaner than Rose had imagined, wiry even. He had long, curly gray hair and a kind, intelligent face that hadn't been diminished by the burn scars to his neck, forehead and around his eyes. If anything, the scarring made him look even wiser, like a blind seer with a sense of humor. But it was clear that he was fully blind. The layout of the downstairs made sense now. "That's an aftershave I've never smelled before—a young man's aftershave. Your son?"

"Yes. This is my Andy, visiting from college."

Hank finished his descent with more confidence, but still grabbing hold of the railing with both hands. At the bottom, he extended his hand to no one in particular. "Pleased to finally meet you, Andy."

"You too, sir." Despite his bemused expression, Andy firmly shook the man's hand.

"And if I'm not mistaken, there's a dark beauty in here somewhere. That fragrance is—"

He halted, mid-sniff, and stood up straight. Sniffed high into the air a few more times as he swiveled this way and that, before finally settling on Rose. Then Bellamy. His cloudy eyes appeared to look through them, past them, between them.

"Don't move," he told Bellamy. With a cautious hand, he felt his way up Bellamy's shirt sleeve to his shoulder, then swept his fingers through that long blond hair, and touched the features of his face with, it seemed to Rose, anticipation bordering on fascination. Rose carefully watched Bellamy's face as he held a calm and cool manner at the total stranger touching him in odd ways. As if he understood the situation beyond what Rose could comprehend. Hank was almost breathless as he shook his head ever so slightly and then stumbled back a step.

"What's wrong?" asked Rose, worried more than puzzled for the first time. She couldn't explain why. "What's the matter?"

"Here, steady yourself on me." Blythe stepped between them, bade Hank to put a hand on her shoulder.

He did. She led him into the living room, leaving Rose and Bellamy to share an incredulous glance. Meanwhile, Andy, who'd taken it upon himself to film the whole scene on his Smartphone, saved the video file and strode after his mom without saying a word, an impish nonchalance shaping his whole manner in a way that infuriated Rose. It was as if he was saying, I told you something was off about your new boyfriend; sucks to be you right now.

"I think—I think I need a glass of water," he stated.

"Mom, what's going on?" Rose asked, pouring a glass of water from a giant jug and handing it to Hank at his request. "What's the deal, Mr. Bonden? You seem to know him from somewhere—Bellamy, I mean."

"Bellamy?" He repeated the name like it meant nothing to him. Pale as the cream-colored walls, he suddenly looked very old, very frail. He trembled all over and was suddenly sweating, the beads gathering on his wrinkled and scarred forehead. "I'll be right," he told her with a peal of forced humor. "We don't get many visitors here is all. I got confused, I guess. Wouldn't be the first time. That deja vu, when it hits, it can open a can of worms. You know what I mean?"

"I know exactly what you mean," Rose replied, watching her mother carefully. "We just visited Greenwood Valley, the site of the old fair. Out of the blue, the memories started flooding in, stuff I'd totally forgotten."

Hank looked alarmed. "You took them to Greenwood Valley?" he addressed Blythe. "Why?"

"It was on the way here. I thought it might help them remember you. Well, Rose, anyway. Andy was just a baby."

"Oh." He finished his water in a few generous gulps, then felt for the table edge with his pinky. The glass shook in his grip, tapped on the varnished surface as he placed it down.

"I can't say I totally remember you, just vague bits and pieces," said Rose, "but Mom sure does. You two were a thing, right?" She might be about as subtle as a jack-hammer to the eardrum, but Rose was done pussy-footing around this mystery. Her mom had promised her answers here, and she wasn't going to wait for them to be eked out.

"So, you told them, Blythe?" He reached out feebly, and when she took his hand, he clasped it with both of his, held it like he'd never let it go. "It's no longer our secret?"

"I told them enough." Blythe threw Andy a quick glance like a mother would to a young child she's willing to behave. She sat on the chair arm beside Hank, poised, not gushing. It told Rose everything she needed to know about this relationship. It had gone unfulfilled for so long, they'd both been reduced to guarding it and nothing more, in their own deeply private ways, so that it was now a cherished, ornamental thing between them. A love thwarted. Trapped in amber, unreachable. It would never again be realized the way it had been once, but it would be always be there.

"So, you've kept in touch all these years?" asked Andy. His sharp tone and childish frown told Rose that their mother's talk with him about the situation didn't go too well. Andy had always been selfish and jealous for their mother's attention. Finding out she'd loved a stranger all these years must have killed him.

But Hank flashed a proud smile, oblivious to Andy's demeanor.

"The fire hit us hard," Blythe explained. "It changed us, changed everything. It was a dark time for both of us, but for Hank most of all. I think we both knew there was no going back after that. We tried, but it didn't work. No need to dig up everything that happened. Some wounds never heal, I guess, but you do learn to live with them. We've always been there for each other. A shoulder to cry on, a friendly voice over the telephone. I helped him learn Braille when he was being stubborn. He gave me good advice when I wanted to quit teaching and become a park ranger in the Yukon."

"That would have been the coolest career switch *ever.*" Andy Foley, future career guidance counselor. For morons.

"No comment," she replied sarcastically.

"But Blythe's been good to me in all sorts of ways she probably hasn't told you about," added Hank. "A few she didn't even tell *me* about. I had to find out for myself. Like when she paid off some of my debts on the farm. A blind farmer isn't exactly going to reap his quota, is he? And when she hired Steph, who's an absolute top dollar home care assistant from Halifax. I'd have been a goner years ago without Steph looking out for me. So, you see what a sweetheart your mother can be...when she gives that encyclopedia brain of hers a rest."

"Hey. I taught history. What do you want? Twitter?"

He snorted a laugh. "It's good to see you. Even though I can't, you know..." his face dropped to his lap.

Blythe leaned over and held his chin up with a gentle cup of her hand. "It's good to see you too,

Mop-head." She then ran a hand through the impressive silver, curly, mop of hair on his head.

It was past shoulder length, big in every sense. But Rose had to admit it suited him. Now that the color had partially returned to his face, she couldn't imagine him any other way. He'd probably always been a character, which would explain why her mom had been drawn to him. She was one herself, the brightest and the best Rose had ever known. And she *got* why these two had remained so close despite everything that had transpired to keep them apart.

They were both comfortable in their own skin. They had the same sense of humor. They were both eccentrics in an increasingly concentric world.

Rose decided she liked this Hank Bonden.

But while she'd focused her attention on them, she'd completely forgotten about Bellamy. He hadn't made a sound since entering, and she wondered what he thought of all this, about Blythe's secret life. How much of this had she told *him,* her professional assistant, confidante, her unaccountably gorgeous accountant?

But, when she looked around, he was gone.

***

The middle bedroom of the three upstairs was also the smallest. And appeared to be the least used. In fact, Rose reckoned nothing had been changed in about fifteen years, since the death of its occupant, Thomas Bonden. Like the rest of the house, it was clean, reasonably dust-free. Thomas' posters—Pulp Fiction, a young, sexy Cameron Diaz, British rock band Oasis, and various biker images—covered most of the wall space. Underneath, the tasteful light blue paint hadn't faded. His trophies for dirt-biking and karate were pristine. Even the cigarette lighter and fingerless biking gloves on his bedside table hadn't been moved. His heavy-duty biker boots stood at the foot of his bed, his jacket, and cut hanging neatly on hangers on the knobs of his armoire.

She half-expected him to march in, pissed off at having to play nice throughout that family outing at the fair with his father's secret girlfriend and her annoying pre-teen daughter. Instead, Bellamy stood over by the window, gazing out over the acres of disused farmland and the graying sky above. What was he thinking about? Why had he come up here, to this specific room?

There was a good photo of him over on the sideboard, posing with his dirt bike and his dad on the passing area of some country lane. He looked especially proud and cocky, and of course insanely cute in his padded riding gear. He'd had shorter hair then. It made him seem even more boyish. Even more...

The sound escaped her throat in a choked whisper. "Bellamy?" The revelation hit Rose like a punch of cold air and she shuddered.

"You're wondering why I look like Thomas Bonden." His voice was flat, professional. He didn't turn from the window. "You want to know why your mother brought us here."

"Let's start with the first one." Her left knee started to wobble; she shifted position to steady herself. "Who are you, really?"

"Bellamy."

"Bullshit. You look *exactly* like this man." She pointed to a photograph. "Not just similar. It's like…

you *are* him."

Bellamy sighed. "I know."

"How do you explain that?" She wasn't even sure if she wanted to know the answer, or if she was ready for it. The whole thing was uncanny. Unnatural.

"I can't. I just happen to look like him."

"You just *happen* to look exactly like the only son, the dead son, of my mom's old boyfriend? Not good enough. What's going on? Why did she bring us here? She knew you looked just like him but she said nothing. What am I missing?" When he didn't reply, Rose took the photo over to him, shoved it in his face. "That's some spooky shit right there. I think you owe me an explanation."

Bellamy cast her a wounded gaze that softened her a little, just enough to accept his hand when he offered it to her.

"You're killing me, Bellamy," she told him, but couldn't decide how she meant the phrase, how deep it went. Humor had always been her defense, but right then she felt wide open, as vulnerable as she'd ever been.

"You've no idea the irony in that statement. Rose,

you're not going to like what I have to say," he replied. Gone was the flat, professional tone. His voice ached with regret, as though he was getting ready to dump her but knew it was going to do more than just break his heart.

"What *is* it, Bellamy? What *is* this secret you've been hiding, you and Mom? Enough is enough."

"I might not be here much longer."

She yanked her hand free from his. The heartache began to spill from her chest, a slow seeping sensation. "What do you mean?"

"I might have to go away."

"Back to England? Texas?"

"No. In my line of work, I travel a lot."

"But you're coming back though, right?"

"If I have to go, I won't be coming back. Not ever."

As she vied with the tears inside her, a bitter fury kept them at bay.

"You son of a bitch!" Rose thumped her fists against his hard chest but he never faltered. "What kind of explanation is that? You never intended to stay around, did you? This whole time, you've been playing me like a goddamn fiddle. Bellamy...you're crushing me. You're breaking my heart. Why?" The urge to punch him repeatedly in the face would have won out...if only she hadn't been holding the photograph under her arm. Thomas Bonden.

She stepped away instead, back to the dresser, where she stood the photo in its original place with a shaking hand. "I don't get it," she continued. "Why's my mom covering for you?"

"She and I—"

"If you mention the words confidential agreement one more time, I swear to God..."

"Rose, all I can say is that Thomas Bonden died fifteen years ago when you were just twelve years old. Your mother brought us here to meet the love of her life before she passes. It means a lot to her that you came, you and Andy. This will be the last trip she ever takes."

"How do you know that? Did she tell you?"

"We talked about it," he replied. "Just like we talked about you, Rose."

"What about me?"

"Your mother doesn't want you to get hurt. The weaker she gets, the more protective of you she becomes. It's impressive, actually."

Rose quickly wiped at a single tear that escaped. "She's strong. Always was. I hope I can be half as strong as she is."

"You are."

Rose rolled her eyes. "But what do you mean, she doesn't want me to get hurt? By you?"

"By what could happen."

Rose pulled a puzzled face, knowing it was one of her most unattractive expressions, but didn't care. "You might as well be tapping out Morse Code, do you know that, right? The way you explain things, even the simplest things, should come with a deciphering handbook. Mom, too. You're geniuses at it, the two of you. But I think I'm onto you. I think I've figured it all out."

He cast her a sharp look. "You have?"

"Uh-huh," she lied. "And if I'm right, it could really change things between us."

Bellamy's face filled with even more sadness, the corners of his eyes drooping to match the frown he wore. "Yes. Unfortunately."

"But as long as Mom's here with us, you won't be

going anywhere."

"True."

"So, we'll just cross that bridge when we come to it." Rose surprised herself with how lightly she could speak of her mom's passing. It wasn't deliberate; it was a survival instinct. Imagining some sort of future with Bellamy, any future, was the only thing keeping her afloat right now. Despair was a hundred anchors dragging her former life away. She had to have *some* hope, a chance at *some* happiness. Life was going to take her beloved mother away, but she thought, until now, that it was giving her Bellamy in return.

"Do you love me, Bellamy?" Her voice spoke with a crack as she held back those unwanted tears. How could she ask that? Expect any sort of reasonable answer from the stranger she'd only just met days ago.

Without hesitation, he proudly replied, "More than I can describe in any earthly way."

"And you want to stay with me? Tell me that much."

The pain and yearning emanating from his glossy eyes were almost too much for her to bear. "I want to stay with you more than anything."

"You swear?"

A lump moved down his throat as he swallowed nervously. "I swear."

She sighed, a little hope restored. "Then…just hold me for a while, okay? Just…no more talk of leaving. You suck at explanations. And I'm tired. So, tired. In here." Massaging over her heart stirred a warmth and a chill at the same time.

Both sensations remained while Bellamy embraced her, but he had that calming effect, that almost supernatural calm about him. It seemed to swallow up all her fears and her hopes in one long, soothing embrace until all she could see was the glare of the sun on the shoulder of an inky cloud. All she could hear was laughter downstairs, her mom's and Hank's. All she could feel was tired. So tired. And something she couldn't describe. Whatever it was, she only felt it when Bellamy was near.

He's not who you think he is, Rose. I just need you to be careful.

Those had been her mom's exact words the night before. Cryptic, just like everything else she'd said about Bellamy, but it was a clear warning *not* to get too involved with him. Why? What was she so afraid of?

A faint aura of moonlight framed the dark curtains. There was no other light in the bedroom. Rose didn't remember falling asleep on Thomas Bonden's bed, but she did recall the sudden, inescapable tiredness that had come over her in Bellamy's embrace. That must have been hours ago. Why hadn't anyone woken her? Were they all spending the night at Hank's? That felt odd to her. Inappropriate somehow.

Noting his absence, she was about to get up to see where Bellamy went, when she sensed him moving across the room. It was like a breath of warm wind that came from nowhere. He made no sound, but there was no mistaking that feeling she got whenever he was close. A million-dollar feeling. One she couldn't get enough of and never wanted to give up.

He came closer. Crouched at the side of the bed, watching her. For some reason, she kept her eyes closed, pretending to remain asleep. Something romantic in that, in knowing that he was secretly watching her, maybe admiring the way she looked. A few strands of hair tickled across her face. Rose hoped it was him caressing her hair, but it could have been a gentle draft blowing through the old farmhouse for how light it was.

Then, he slowly stood up and left the room, leaving Rose wanting but unable to call after him. His footsteps along the landing were soft, measured. The floorboards didn't creak, but they should have; Bellamy weighed a lot more than Rose, and they'd creaked under her. It was pitch black out there. Black and silent like the back of a deep, forbidden cave. He made his way toward the stairs, not to the bathroom as she assumed. She listened hard but couldn't hear the voices below. No TV either. Were they all asleep? *Where* were they sleeping?

Rose suddenly had to know. The PI in her was wide awake and playful. Did he want to sneak around a strange house in the dark? Two could play at that game. She took her boots off and set them gently on the carpet.

He's not who you think he is, Rose. I just need you to be careful.

He loved her. That was obvious. However crazy that may sound. And Mom trusted him enough to spend so much of her precious time with him. So, what did

Rose have to be careful about? What *was* all this nonsense? How futile to believe she would get answers in coming here. All she gained were more questions.

Rose tiptoed downstairs, hugging the right side of the steps. Quieter than she'd been in years. She felt like she could walk on water. At the bottom, the rec room, adjacent to the living room, was occupied. The TV was on in there, but the sound was off. Her mom and Andy were asleep on the sofa, an empty bucket of popcorn on its side between them. He'd covered her with his jacket and his feet were up on the coffee table.

Rose entered the living room, immediately spied Bellamy's crouched shape in front of Hank's armchair. Faint scribbling light from the TV in the next room reflected off the wall over the fireplace hearth to Hank's right; the opposite half of the room sat completely dark. Rose sneaked closer, took up a crouching position at the side of a china cabinet. She was hidden there, but she could hear the two of them talking.

She could hear every word.

"You know, I was in your room—Tom's room, I mean—shortly before you arrived. I hadn't been in there in ages. Something just made me want to feel what it was like again, to remember what he was like. A blind man sees the past more clearly, I reckon. Do you think I knew somehow that you were coming, like a sixth sense kind of a thing? My eyesight went, so I developed a touch of foresight?"

"Possibly. One's senses sharpen in unexpected ways in anticipation of death. I've seen it before, Hank."

Rose's breath caught in her throat at the sound of Bellamy speak the word death. Was he going to hurt Hank?

"But it's not a fear thing. I want you to know that. When I recognized you—Tom, I mean—in the hallway earlier, I wasn't afraid. I just didn't expect it. I didn't expect *him*. My boy."

"I understand. And I want you to know, I never choose the form I take."

"Oh? Who does?"

"No one knows. It appears to be pre-selected but always has a purpose. I see now, the meaning of this one. Of Thomas."

"Oh." Hank mulled that idea over before he gave his grave reply, "I guess there's a certain logic to it. That it was supposed to make this easier."

"Is it...making this easier?"

"Not really. It just begs more questions. Like why *Tom* hasn't come to fetch me himself. Why send someone made up to look like Tom? It's...confusing. It hurts."

"I'm sorry for that," replied Bellamy, as tenderly as honestly as anything Rose had heard him say. "I'm here to make you feel as comfortable as possible before your journey."

"My journey." Hank's breathless whisper echoed inside her deepest fears.

Just what did they mean by a journey? Was this some pre-arranged assisted suicide thing? Was her *mom* in on it? Maybe *that* was Bellamy's specialty: a professional euthanizer, a Dr. Kevorkian for hire. Maybe her mom wanted the same treatment and she'd come here to die with Hank, they'd made this arrangement beforehand.

Rose ran the idea back over the events of the past few days, couldn't get it to fit except in the most superficial ways. It would explain Bellamy's anonymity, the so-called "client confidentiality" he shared with Blythe, the dark, mysterious side to his character, and the fact that he'd gotten to know so many people despite his young age. But it did not explain why her mom had had him hanging around like this, almost as part of the family, and had let him spend so much time with Rose, whom he'd obviously had his eye on as soon as they'd met. Nor did it explain the encounter with the gunman.

Or the fact that he just said he doesn't control the form he takes.

For the first time, she considered the impossible. But perhaps, she'd just been fighting the idea this whole time. This man she'd fallen for in just aa handful of hours, could he be someone, *something*...unprecedented? As in...not human?

"Will it take long?" asked Hank, gripping Bellamy by the shoulders as their foreheads touched.

"Not even a moment of earthly time. But it will be an adventure. I've guided many souls across the In-Between, and those who know themselves best seem to have greater experiences. Let go of this world, but be sure to take the best parts of it with you. Hold onto them deep inside, and let them color your place in the Great Beyond."

"You've been there, Bellamy? You've seen what it's like?"

"I've never had the privilege of seeing it. The In-Between is my domain. I'm neither alive nor a part of the Great Beyond. It's my sacrifice for mankind. But you have a place there, Hank. You've led a good life."

"I've made mistakes..."

"Everyone has. Don't dwell on them. Every adventure has its setbacks, but we learn to overcome them. You can use that knowledge on your next adventure."

"I think I like that idea, Bellamy." The old man quivered then. "I always did like reading adventure stories. If I hadn't lost my boy and my sight, and my Blythe...who knows what I could've done."

"And what you can yet do. Focus on that, Hank. Focus on who and what you want to find waiting for you in the Great Beyond and it will be there."

"Then I don't want to wait any longer. I have it all right here." He pressed a hand to his heart. "You're sure they'll all be there waiting? You said you've never been there yourself."

"I have insight. It tells me a man like you has nothing to worry about and everything to look forward to."

"In that case, I'm ready. And thank you…for everything."

Bellamy smiled. "You're welcome."

"You'll take care of my Blythe, then?"

"Of course. She's the whole reason I came in the first place."

At that, Rose slinked down to the floor, unable to hold herself up in her hiding place. Tears sprang from her eyes and drenched her face before pooling in the crease of her neck. So, it was true. But Rose had to see it with her own eyes to truly believe it. Wiping her face with her shirt sleeve, she then peered around the cabinet once more to watch the man she loved take Hank's life.

"Now, concentrate on my voice. Everything is about to go dark," he explained. "Darker than a dreamless sleep. Let it take you. Drift into its embrace. Imagine it's guiding you along with the current of a cosmic river, a current you've in fact been on your whole life. It will lead you to the Great Beyond, the glittering shore that awaits you there. I'll be by your side until the first light of the Great Beyond flickers across the darkness. When I leave, others will take my place to help guide you the rest of the way. That is the end of my domain and the beginning of yours..."

Rose watched, stunned, as the dark fixtures of the room came alive, their outlines briefly lit by some sort of ultraviolet afterglow. A weak camera flash in slow motion. The shapes of the two men faded away inside the radiance as though they'd belonged to it all along, as though it had come back to collect them. When the darkness returned, Bellamy was gone and Hank was slumped in his armchair, unmoving, lifeless.

"Bellamy!" she croaked, the attempt to shout only a strained whisper.

She crawled out of her hiding place and knelt there, upright on the carpet, wondering why she couldn't seem to buy what had just happened. Like an overreaching dream during a short power nap, her brain resisted it. Told her it was something impressive and fanciful while it lasted but that she had it under control. She needn't fear it. Reality had her by the hand and would guide her out of this craziness, right?

She managed to get to her feet, wandered through the eerie silence. No ticking of a clock. No snoring from the other room. No crickets outside. It felt like Rose and the old house were holding their breaths simultaneously, waiting for her to wake up. But she didn't. This wasn't like any dream she remembered having, but it wasn't real, either. Couldn't be. Shakily, she shuffled towards Hank's body and reached out to feel his pulse.

Gone.

With that confirmation, Rose made her way back to the stairs with a vague plan to rouse herself from the bed in Tom Bonden's room. It felt weird, but it was all she had. Deep pangs of sadness and loneliness and betrayal weighed her down as she reached the hallway and looked to the front door, imagining a desolate dream world beyond, a dream she might never wake from.

That idea frightened her, rooted her to the foot of the stairs, and made climbing them feel impossible. It was an anchor on her heart, that idea she'd probably never get to see those closest to her ever again if she didn't wake up. She sat on the bottom step, hugging the wooden railing post, praying she didn't have to endure this dream, this nightmare, any longer. Losing Bellamy and her mom at the same time, whether it was real or not, was poison she had no antidote for. A fatal dose of truth and possibility. Suddenly, waking or not waking were equally nightmarish.

She sat there, pressed against the cool wood, lost. All the logic and reason and snark she relied on in her work had deserted her. Trying to summon them was like sucking in a deep breath at high altitude; she was someplace she shouldn't be.

"I told you, he's not who you think he is, Rose."

She thought at first it was the voice in her head, repeating what her mom had said about Bellamy. But when she glanced up, her mom was standing there, wrapping her shawl around herself. A look of unfussy focus suggested Blythe knew something about what had happened, and maybe what to do next.

"Mom? Where am I? Why can't I breathe?"

"You saw something, didn't you?" But it wasn't a question. "And now they're gone."

"I-I saw *him* vanish, right in front of me." Rose thought for a second, remembered the slumped figure in the armchair. "But Hank's still there." She swallowed. "Isn't he?"

Blythe sighed, shook her head. "I'm afraid not, Rosie. You saw more than you were supposed to, but I think maybe it's better this way."

"What do you mean? Why can't I wake up?"

"Because you're already awake. Here, I think you'd better come with me. No more secrets, I swear." She offered her arm. It was likely the only gesture that would have gotten Rose to her feet. If anyone could guide her through this living nightmare, it was her beloved mother, who'd seen her through all the darkest times of her life. As long as they were together, Rose knew things would turn out okay.

"Where are we going?" she asked, opening the front door for them both. It was a little chilly out, but Rose still had her jacket on.

"Let's go for a walk," said Blythe.

"In the middle of the night?"

"Sure. It's more peaceful at this time. No distractions. We can talk all we want." She pinched the two halves of the shawl together under her chin.

"Um, okay. But do you know your way around? There's only moonlight out there."

Blythe closed her eyes and sighed happily up at the sky. "Moonlight is perfect."

"If you say so."

Walking arm-in-arm with her mom down a strange country lane, past midnight, just the two of them alone for what seemed like forever in every direction, would have been the most magical thing in the world for Rose once upon a time. But she was not herself right now. Too many shocks and unanswered questions over the past few days had taken their toll. They hadn't even reached the line of trees that marked the start of Hank's driveway and followed the adjoining road around to the east when the moon disappeared behind a thicket of clouds. Rose literally couldn't see the ground below her feet.

Luckily, she remembered her cell phone had a light. When she switched it on, it produced an odd tunnel effect, lighting the two of them and the ground ahead fairly well, but it barely reached the low stone walls on either side. The result was haunting and intimate.

"He's not who you think he is. That was what you said to me last night," Rose reminded Blythe. "What I just saw definitely fits that description. But I need you to *tell* me what I just saw. I need to hear the words spoken out loud. Mom, who *is* he?"

"He came for me, sweetie. Three nights ago, he came because it was my time. I had a heart attack. I should have died. When Bellamy arrived, he just appeared from out of the shadows in the room, said he was there to help me pass on, to take me to somewhere he calls the Great Beyond. He's Death, Rose. The man we call Bellamy is the Bringer of Death, a carrier of souls to the afterlife. He was summoned to take me like he'd been summoned to take countless other souls over the centuries."

She heard the words but didn't really take them in. Couldn't. She was outside herself listening in, a third party in this tunnel of light through the darkness. The words couldn't hurt her while she was like this. She was skeptical but unable to analyze. Guarded but unarmed. What her mom said had to be true because too many extraordinary things had happened over the past few days and only an extraordinary explanation, even a frightening one, would do them justice. But if it was all true, it also meant that Bellamy was gone.

"Why didn't he take you?"

"Because he saw you, Rose. He saw you in that photo I keep on my little table."

Something hit her right in the gut. "What? Why should that..." But she knew, knew how it all fit, knew why he'd stayed with Blythe long after her allotted time had expired. "He wants to stay, doesn't he? He wants to give up...whatever it was he was doing."

"What he wants…is to be with you, Rosie."

A longing stirred inside her, spread as far as the fear would let it, maybe even a little further. "He was like us once. Alive, I mean. He told me so—in his own roundabout way." The vision Rose had that evening on the roof, after gazing into his eyes, the twin circlets aflame, jolted her with realization. *That* had been his memory, serving on a ship during the Battle of the Nile. He'd sacrificed himself to save his captain's life, had fallen overboard...to his death. Bellamy had given her a piece of the puzzle right there, maybe the most crucial one of all. "Whatever he's done since then, it's because he was chosen," she mused. "You saw how he was with Hank. How he helped reassure him, set him at ease before his journey. He's a good man, Rosie. You chose a good man."

"Who just happens to be *Death*? Boy, can I pick 'em or what?"

"Don't forget he picked you, too. He was ready to give it all up at just the mere sight of you. He just didn't know how."

"I don't understand that part. He's not...I mean *how* can he give it up? He died three hundred years ago."

"Like I said, he didn't even know if it was possible. He just knew he had to try," explained Blythe.

"But the reason he came here—for you, I mean. Has he given you a second chance or something? Some kind of reprieve?" Rose prayed to hear the word *permanent*.

"He gave me some more time, yes."

"In exchange for what?"

"In exchange for him staying with me and experiencing what it's like to be alive. He'd forgotten."

"Yeah. I kinda noticed. But he damn sure didn't forget how to—" Rose cleared her throat, embarrassed. "So, where does that leave us? What happens now?"

"The riddle still has to be answered."

"The riddle of..."

"Life from death."

"Give it to me," said Rose, loosening her shoulders and her neck muscles in preparation. She'd always been pretty good at solving puzzles, just not when they were problems in her own life. And this had to be the most important riddle of her life.

"By some unearthly intervention, you love each other. Knowing what you now know, do you still want to be with him?"

Rose hesitated, she knew that weighing up the revelations of the past few days with any kind of logic would be impossible. She could spend a lifetime trying to get to the bottom of this dilemma and not fully understand it. Not even if every minute facet of Bellamy's otherworldly role were explained to her. It really boiled down to this: what she ought to do, what most people would do, and what would leave her—Rose Foley—with the fewest regrets.

"I just can't help but think of you and Hank," she replied. "He's your biggest regret, isn't he—that you missed all that time with him when you should have been together."

Blythe didn't respond right away. By the time she did, with a nod, Rose was completely and ridiculously lost. The walls had disappeared and they seemed to be climbing a dirt track up a ridgeline. She hoped her cell phone's battery had enough power to get them back.

"About Hank—did you know he was going to die tonight?" Rose asked her mom. "Did Bellamy tell you?"

"He didn't tell me. But I knew. Not right away, but I should have figured it out when Bellamy first appeared as Hank's son, Thomas. That day Thomas died in the fire, it's the epicenter of all this. It was the turning point in all our lives. I had my first heart attack, almost died. Hank lost his eyesight trying to save his boy. And that day was the only time you'd have seen Thomas, who looked exactly like the man you've fallen in love with. Bellamy appearing as Thomas Bonden was the key to the big riddle. He was a boy I hardly knew; but he meant the world to Hank. The more I considered the importance of that, the more I came to realize, Bellamy was summoned here to take *Hank*."

"Not you? I thought you said he appeared to you three nights ago?"

"He did. But I think it all happened for a reason. I think everything does. His seeing your picture, wanting to meet you, giving me more time so that he could get close to you; then his willingness to defy fate itself in order to find a way to stay with you. I think that was all planned for him, to give him what he desperately wants."

"And what's that?"

"A second chance at life. He's fulfilled his cosmic duty and now they want to give him this chance to be happy again."

"How do *you* know all this, Mom?"

Blythe placed a reassuring hand on her daughter's shoulder, then glanced up to the gibbous moon as it breached the gray swathe of clouds. "Did I mention he volunteered?"

"No," answered Rose. "But I figured he must have, the way he gave his life for his captain like that. It's in his nature, I guess. To help those in trouble."

"He referred to it as his calling."

"Uh-huh. But he couldn't have been the first to get that calling, right? He died at the end of the eighteenth century; there must have been others like him throughout history up until that time, right?"

Blythe grinned. "That's my girl."

"Other volunteers before him," Rose went on. "Which means he had to have replaced someone. *He got the calling because someone else*—his predecessor—quit. Or got fired."

"I somehow doubt pink slips are involved."

"You know what I mean. The point is…it's possible! It makes sense, given what came before. It means he doesn't have to be bound to it forever. As long as someone else gets the calling...or better still…volunteers?"

"You always were my smart little girl." Her mother lifted a hand to cup Rose's face in her palm, the way she always did when Rose was a child.

Once again, tears forced their way through her eyes but this time Rose let them. "I had a good teacher."

"So, my sweet child, have you answered the riddle yet?"

"Which one?"

"Knowing what you know, do you still want to be with him?"

A quietly thrilling surge of hope made Rose want to cheer out loud. Instead, she kept it together. "I think you know the answer to that."

No reply. She went to nudge her mom but realized that their arms weren't linked anymore. Had she fallen? Rose shone her light on the ground behind her, fearing the worst. But her mom wasn't there. Not on the dirt path. Not in the long grass lining the right side. Nor in the shallow ditch lining the left.

"Mom!"

No answer.

"Mom, where are you?"

There was no reply. Panic set in. She frantically searched and searched but could find no sign of her mom. Retracing their steps past more than a few hundred yards did no good because she didn't know how they'd reached the dirt path in the first place.

"*Mom!*"

She searched until first light, and when she glimpsed Hank's farmhouse in the distance, so far away—who knows how long they'd been walking in the dark—

Rose found the path they'd taken and followed it back. But she found no sign of her mom.

Not until she entered the house and found Blythe lying there, curled up on the sofa next to Andy, an empty bucket of popcorn still on its side between them. He'd covered her with his jacket, and his feet were still up on the coffee table. Her shawl was nowhere to be seen. It appeared as though they hadn't moved at all since earlier that night when Rose first spotted them there.

But how could that be?

Rose bent to rouse her mom. But as she got close enough to whisper, an icy realization washed over her. Her heart fell. Blythe *hadn't* moved since earlier that night. And she wasn't moving now.

Death had already taken her.

CHAPTER TWELVE

Over the next few weeks, Rose often doubted her own sanity, painfully, and in-depth. It didn't help that Andy kept cutting her off whenever she turned the subject toward the supernatural during their phone conversations. He knew their mom had gone to see Hank one last time before she died; that she had died there was plausible, given her weak condition. And Hank's home care worker, Steph, had confirmed how ill he had been lately—he was prone to aneurisms, had been on beta-blockers and other assorted medication for years. It was therefore not out of the realm of possibility, given the strong emotions Blythe's visit had stirred, that he'd also died of natural causes the exact same night.

To the pathologist and the coroner and everyone else, it was a coincidence, albeit an unusual one. But Rose knew differently. Her mom had officially died about two hours *before* Hank and, yet, she and her mom had taken that walk *after* she'd seen Hank die. It made no sense unless the explanation was supernatural. Mom couldn't have been walking with her and, yet…she had been. For hours. Telling her everything she knew. If that wasn't proof of life after death then what about Bellamy? *He'd* vanished before her eyes and had never reappeared after. No trace of him anywhere. It was like he'd never existed. Even now, weeks later.

Andy maintained he didn't know what had happened to Bellamy and didn't want to know. Whatever mom had hired him for, it was over with now. At least he no longer believed Bellamy's motives had been unsavory; Blythe had set him straight on that score. But he flat-out refused to buy into Rose's Ouija talk.

People die. People lie. Show me some solid proof or else it's all just wishful thinking. Honestly, I didn't think you were like that, Rosie. I thought you knew better than that.

And she had once, before Bellamy. But the more she pitted the facts of those three days against the so-called wishful thinking, the more she realized that it was impossible to prove any of it, at least anything supernatural. All she had was her own experience, and that told her everything her mom had said on that inexplicable midnight walk was true. It buoyed her with hope, knowing that somewhere, Bellamy and her mom were waiting for her, maybe watching on, maybe even reaching out to help her every now and then.

But with hope came sadness. A deep, broad ocean of sadness on which hope could only stay afloat for so long before reality drowned it again. The reality that said here, now, and for the rest of her life she was going to be without the only two people she couldn't stand to be without.

Bellamy had tried and failed to break free from his otherworldly duties in order to stay with her. She cried whenever she imagined him trying. Maybe he was trying still, somewhere, railing against the higher powers as he pictured Rose, in whichever ways he remembered her, desperately fighting the impossible fight against death and fate. That idea would always make her cry.

Always.

Then she'd lost her mom. Those tears needed no explanation, no rationale. But the thing that upset her most, that continued to nag at her weeks later when she returned to her mom's apartment to start boxing up her personal effects, was how helpless she felt. How utterly freaking ineffectual. Mom had died, Hank had died, Bellamy had vanished from her life, and she hadn't been able to prevent any of it. It had all just happened right there in front of her, like watching someone just fall from a cliff and you're unable to jump after them. The most important things ever to have happened to her and all she could do was watch. These people she loved had been fighting the most powerful forces in the universe and all she'd done was think of herself, how selfish *they* were being for not including *her*.

She flipped through her mom's diary, ready to just toss it into the box. She leafed straight to the dog-eared final entry, glimpsed the name "Rose" several times, and had to sit down before forcing herself to read. Painful to relive that final day, but maybe it would help to know her mom's true state of mind before the fateful road trip.

Dearest Rose,

If what I've imagined happening is about to happen, this will be the last thing I ever get to write. Know that I write it thinking of you, only you, as I have thought of you these past few bittersweet days we've spent together.

I will die tomorrow night. There is no getting around that. I don't want it, I don't welcome it, and there is little comfort in knowing for certain that there is life after death. But there must be life after death. Bellamy is proof of that. He is not of this world, Rose, though he was once. When he died, he was called upon and offered an extraordinary duty and he accepted it with grace, which he has done for centuries. He guides the souls of the deceased across to the Great Beyond, as he calls it. He came to guide me.

But tonight, I had a revelation, you might even say a calling. You see, Bellamy has unfinished business with our world, with the life that was cut short from him. He yearns to live again, with the woman he loves. That woman is you, Rose. He chose you the first instant he saw your picture. I believe Fate intervened to bring you together. Just as I believe he came to me, because now it is my turn to help him, and by that, I really mean help you both find the happiness you deserve.

I never did feel like I was ready to retire. This way I guess I don't have to. It's calling me, Rose—adventure is calling me. I don't know how it works or who I answer to exactly. All I know is that I have to choose. Bellamy chose, and he saw the wonders of the universe. But my reason for choosing is far simpler and far more important to me: it will give you this chance to be happy. When I'm gone, be kind to him. If he isn't there with you, go find him. Never stop looking. Don't let doubt stop you. Find him and keep him and make a life together. Do what Hank and I could not. And always remember, this was meant to be.

With all my love,

Mom

***

The cries of seagulls and the intoxicating scent of sea air accompanied her every step of the way through historic Portsmouth town as she strolled, as if in a dream, parallel to the ancient-looking stone wall protecting the old town from the sea, toward her rendezvous. Passing quaint, cobbled side streets, she enjoyed the smell of beer from the pubs and especially the aroma of fish and chips.

Six thousand miles from home, Rose felt strangely comfortable here. It may have been memories of her mom reading her stories of British naval history, some of them amazingly detailed and specific, conjuring images and vibes that translated in subtle ways to the sights and smells and the ambiance of what she was experiencing now, decades later. That idea took the edge off her grief. Several weeks had passed since her mom had died, and not an hour had gone by when Rose hadn't thought of her, of what her mother had said on that eerie midnight walk and in her final diary entry, with a crazy mix of emotions.

Most of all, Rose just missed having her there, her best friend, her anchor. The mysterious events surrounding her mom's passing merely added fog to a time in her life she already couldn't see clearly, objectively. What it all meant. Why it had happened to *them*. Rose believed everything her mom had said but she still couldn't make a reality out of it. Too much of it was ineffable. Far-reaching. Impossible to get her head around.

So, she'd focused all her energy on solving the only problem she even had a hope of solving, one for which her investigative skills came in handy. Her mother's written word ringing in her mind: *If he isn't there with you, go find him. Never stop looking.*

With her mom's words in her heart, Rose had pursued every possible path she could think of to track him down; police missing person reports, social media campaigns, facial recognition software in case he didn't know who he was and someone had helped him by posting his photo online. For all of these, she used the images her partner Alex had taken when he'd been following Bellamy. Working closely with those— pretty much the only real proof that Bellamy had even existed—had lit a fire under her, had made Rose absolutely determined to find him. If he was alive at all, she would track him down.

She'd even contacted the British Admiralty archives to see if they had any information on a young sailor who'd served and died under Nelson at the Battle of the Nile. All she had was his first name, Bellamy, a possible surname, Smith, and his wife's name, Alice. The curator had emailed back saying he would look into it personally, but a couple of weeks had passed before Rose had received her first solid lead. It wasn't from the Admiralty archives, but it was from England. From somewhere called Southsea, to be precise, not far from Portsmouth.

A police inspector there had picked up a confused young man in his mid-twenties, who'd been wandering around on the beach. He didn't seem to know who he was, where he was from, or what year it was. He also had no ID, no passport—he spoke with an odd American accent—and had no money. So, the inspector had contacted the US Embassy, who in turn had checked the usual channels, probably the same ones Rose had used to get the word out in the first place and had identified him as the missing man in her adverts. Then they'd called her cell phone while she was in a bath one night. After furiously stumbling out naked and covered with soap, she'd managed to brow-beat several high-ranking diplomats and red-tape sticklers, and convinced them to let her fly over and see him in person before it went any further.

She'd sent the Southsea inspector's office enough money to put Bellamy up in a local bed and breakfast for a few days, and provide him with some spending money until she could get there. God, the anticipation. Rose willed the plane to move faster, pulling the land towards them with her mind. Her body ached to be with him. She needed him. And the thought, the slight chance that he could be alive…

"It's all quite irregular and very much against the rules, Miss, but seeing as this so-called Bellamy was a polite enough bloke who hadn't caused anyone any trouble, why, it seemed a shame to keep him locked up when all he wanted was to get some fresh air and wait for his American sweetheart to come to fetch him. He couldn't remember her name, but he'd gone on and on about mint chocolate chip ice cream and an island in the middle of a harbor. Funny really, how he'd been able to remember some things so clearly and other things, like names, not at all."

The sun began to dip behind the masts and sails of expensive yachts cruising into Portsmouth harbor from the Solent. It wasn't especially busy on the wharves, not as much as Rose had expected. It was full of tourists, however, who glanced around them much as she did. Still, the harbor was everything Rose had hoped it to be and more: her mom would have just loved the museums and the old stone buildings and the big ships, whether restored antiques or new battleships, dotted around. It gave her a sense of history not just being some remote and distant thing, but all around her and constantly infusing every aspect of modern life. All things had roots, were connected to other things that had preceded them. Mom would love that idea, that Rose not only thought it but felt it in her bones.

And always remember, this was meant to be.

She found Pier F and eagerly scanned the line of people waiting for the next Harbor Sightseeing Cruise. He'd be there right about now; the innkeeper had told Rose when she called ahead. Apparently, he was bustling all morning, unable to sit at the inn, and wait. He left a note for Rose to meet him at the pier. But she couldn't find him anywhere on the wharf.

There were two ferry-type boats on their way back in to dock. Bellamy must have been on one of those, maybe he went out for a cruise while he waited for her. The flutter in her stomach that had persisted ever since she'd landed at Heathrow, now swarmed into a breathless, giddy excitement. The mysteries of the past several weeks all seemed to be churning in the wake of the slowly reversing ship. Possibly, somewhere on there was a man who should not, by the known laws of nature, exist. A man whose love she should not, by any common sense, share. But he did, and she did, and if for no other reason, that was all the proof Rose needed that things really did happen for a reason. That nothing was impossible. If love could conquer Death, then neither she nor Bellamy, or even her mom, would ever be without it.

The ship docked just as it had done thousands of times before, in the same spot on the dock, after the same routine cruise around the same harbor. But in Rose's mind, it was the end of a voyage that had been left unfinished for centuries. A homecoming for a brave young sailor whose sense of duty had led him beyond life and death to places no one had ever dreamed of. In her mind, she was the girl he'd imagined coming home to. She might not have freckles or a bonnet or a damn frilly umbrella, but she did have knee-high boots and rocked a black leather jacket in a way that said she *knew* what it was like to be an outsider, someone who didn't belong and more importantly didn't give a heck about much. She was who he needed in this new century, this new life he'd been gifted.

A hundred tourists disembarked, but her eyes scanned and only saw one. And he only saw her. Gone was the faintly bemused expression he'd had that day at her mom's when they'd first met. He rocked a little on the gangway as it moved, had to hold on tight to the rope. He was no longer a force of nature with omnipotent powers.

Surely, over the past few weeks, he'd had to engage with the world all over again, with its consequences, its nitty-gritty, like one of those Greek gods in her mom's stories who'd perhaps looked down on mortal affairs until he'd had to assume human form and seen firsthand that life wasn't some sweeping grandiose design; it was all about the little things, the mistakes, the course-corrections, the messy human connections, the snatched joys and fleeting glimpses of dreams-come-true, the regrets and the wisdom that came from managing those regrets.

Like her mom had been Rose's anchor, Rose would have to be Bellamy's, at least for a while. She smiled at the thought. She'd never been anyone's anchor before, and it made her feel older, but not old. She had a responsibility now, unlike anyone else's in the world. How much did he remember about his supernatural adventures? What could he tell her about the Great Beyond? But more than that, what could she do to make him happy?

They'd only been on one official date and already he was the least boring boyfriend she'd ever had. Rose was glad he'd kept the long hair and the boyish biker look. But that natty turtleneck sweater would have to go. Then she glanced down at her black tank top with the Punisher logo on the front. She'd hope it would jog more of his memory, but it was showing a fair bit of cleavage. She suddenly felt self-conscious, picturing the conservative fashions of his time. Rose then pulled the halves of her jacket together for the sake of modesty, then thought about it and rolled her eyes.

Play by your own rules, Rosie, she could almost hear her

mom saying. *You only get one shot at this, so make it count.*

"I'm looking for a lost sailor, used to live around here," she called to him as he began to approach.

The flash of a grin warmed her belly.

"Oh? Sounds like you've come a long way to find him," he replied.

She shrugged. "You could say that."

"I used to know a man who fit that description. He was at sea for a long time. Word is, he was rescued by a beautiful and mysterious nymph with raven hair."

"Yeah, a Canadian girl. I think I know her. They lived happily ever after, right? After she showed him who was boss, I mean."

He laughed. "No doubt they had fun while she tried."

"Uh-huh. I think you'd better come over here, stranger. Let me get a better look at you."

He locked his gaze on hers and approached along the edge of the wharf with a smoldering singlemindedness. He seemed to want her in all the ways she'd imagined, in all the ways she wanted him. When their bodies met, Rose's arms took a life of their own and wrung their fingers through his golden hair, something she'd been dying to do for weeks. He leaned in, a soft and warm breath tickled her face, and she met his kiss and the subtle taste of a sweet sea breeze with an eager, exploring one of her own.

"About this sailor you're looking for," he whispered in her ear just before he kissed her neck.

Rose closed her eyes in ecstasy. "You'll do."

The End

ABOUT THE AUTHOR

#1 International and USA TODAY Bestselling Author, Candace Osmond was born in North York, ON. She's also an Award-winning Screenwriter. Candace currently resides on the rocky east coast of Canada with her husband, two kids, and bulldog.

Connect with Candace online! She LOVES to hear from readers! *www.AuthorCandaceOsmond.com*